Unbound

PRENTICE-HALL, INC., Englewood Cliffs, N. J.

Jones Unbound by Walter Lockwood
Copyright © 1973 by Walter Lockwood

Printed in the United States of America

Prentice-Hall International, Inc., London
Prentice-Hall of Australia, Pty. Ltd., North Sydney
Prentice-Hall of Canada, Ltd., Toronto
Prentice-Hall of India Private Ltd., New Delhi
Prentice-Hall of Japan, Inc., Tokyo

10 9 8 7 6 5 4 3 2 1

Library of Congress Cataloging in Publication Data

Lockwood, Walter
  Jones unbound.

  I. Title.
PZ4.L8225Jo [PS3562.O294] 813'.5'4 72–12740
ISBN 0–13–510065–8

1734124

To Hargas,
whose insanity has helped

Jones Unbound

1

Fielding Jones had just finished the last page of a nasty letter to the Elders when his wife, with a little gasp from out in the kitchen, dropped a beer glass into the garbage disposal and noisily collapsed. Knowing that she disliked an untidy desk, even in his study, he quickly scattered the penned sheets, nudged writing implements onto the carpet, tipped an ashtray, and went in to find her cold on their Turkish mosaic floor.

"Sarah," he cried. "My God, we're to go to the Dean's tonight."

Then, struggling for breath, he removed her English dustcap and touched her forehead.

"Poor Sarah. Good Lord, died with dirty feet. Not even a chance to get a shower. Gone spotless to every occasion but this." And thinking of what his mother might say, he added, "Dear God, life is a vale of tears."

And the sun gleamed warm on the face of the barometer from his great-grandfather's Glasgow pub, announcing the glory of an early April evening.

". . . and her saintly life shall earn her just reward, for to the godly go the spoils of heaven. This earth, overwhelmed by the unjust, the obscene, the smut of life, can find joy and hope in this glowing example of God's grace. Her word, her deed were one—cleanness, holiness guided her life. We mourn the dearly departed, but we should not mourn. For we view life from our vale of tears while she gazes down upon us from the sunlit mountain peak."

Cleanness guided her life all right. Reverend DeGlopper knew. Clean as a cat's ass. But she had her smutty moments, God bless her for those. Short hop between Calvinist and pagan. At least for Sarah. A tongue could be her undoing. Old Sarah. I'll miss your sweet smell. But I'll manage. It's April and I'll manage.

Charles Jones, brilliant and semiliterate half-hippie, pushed his wild locks out of his eyes and took his father's arm.

"I'll miss her, Fielding."

Jones, hunched over and still ten inches taller than his son, covered the hand with his own huge hammy paw, as the sun warmed Sarah's little house.

"Let's have a drink."

Charles looked up at him, eyes dreary, bloodshot. "We shouldn't."

"We should."

"But the reception . . ."

"Hang it, Charles. I haven't seen you for eighteen months. When do you leave?"

"I have to be back in Denver tomorrow night, Fielding. But . . ."

"Dammit, Charles. Come home with me. You're always

2

going somewhere. If there's grief to be shared, I want it to be with you and not some pontificating Dutch minister."

Charles had trouble swallowing. "I'm pretty much off the stuff. This doesn't seem like the time."

"Never a better time. The Irish are barbarians, but civilized when it comes to funerals. If someone has passed out of the vale of tears and climbed atop Olympus, they do the only sane thing—they celebrate. I'm not suggesting an orgy, Charles. You could come cry in a beer with me. I'm forty-eight now; there's time for only a few. Tears, I mean."

"All right, Fielding. I'll explain to Reverend DeGlopper."

He walked down the path to the Reverend's humble Oldsmobile. Jones stood alone with eight inches of concrete and steel between the flesh. Alone with a gouge in the earth. Need to make mine deeper than this. There'll be a stench to cover them. Call in the sanitary landfill.

Good-bye, Sarah. Sweet Sarah. Stay chaste till I come for you. And mind you've got God cleaning his fingernails. Hanging out the sheets. There'll be hell to pay in heaven, Lord, now Sarah's arrived.

2

The sun poured red through French windows and transparent film of curtains. The April sun was new and plump as fruit. Beside the fieldstone fireplace Jones stood, prodding a flickering pile of bituminous coal. Charles sat in a rocker in his blue jeans, nursing a Canadian, sorting through a ratty photo album. Three days dead and the house was already comfortably disordered. Dust on the books. Glass in the disposal. A sardine can on the mantlepiece. All things where he left them. A man's house for the first time.

"Why do you burn that?" Charles reverently closed the album and placed it on the top of the grand piano.

"What, son? The coal you mean?"

"It's heavy stuff. Sulfurous. A serious pollutant, I mean."

"Oh, it is? No, I didn't know. It's very cheap. Cheap fuel is good fuel."

"Not necessarily."

"Okay, Charles."

Looking hurt, Charles poured himself another.

"Come on, son. This whole affair has been a tremendous blow . . ."

"I know, Fielding. Wow. I still can't believe it. Why her, of all people?"

Jones poked coal, cursing for fire.

"Sarah was better prepared than most."

"True. Mother experienced as true a conversion as anyone ever has."

"Certainly did."

Sip it, Charles. That's not to be swilled like orange crush. Dammit, the only bottle left in the house. Drinks like a Calvinist—every glass as if it's the last.

"My own metamorphosis was a powerful experience." Charles grinned mysteriously, crossing his legs neat as barber's scissors.

"Mine too."

"Yours?"

"The moment of your conception, son. It wasn't exactly immaculate—but certainly one of the more joyful ones."

"Christ, Fielding."

"Not to speak ill of the dead."

"I wasn't conceived. You adopted me."

"Oh? Oh, yes. So we did. I'd forgotten."

Charles turned his back and brought his fist down on the grand piano. It rang a low G.

"Dammit. You've always made light of every serious situation we've confronted. You refuse to be serious about things that are deadly serious. Life isn't a joke. Hell . . . why, you don't even seem sorry that mother is dead. I know that's brutal to say, but it's true. Don't you feel anything? Any pain? Any sorrow? Why is everything so funny to you?"

6

Jones leaned the poker on a stone and looked at his son. Longest speech he'd ever heard from him. Always suspected his mother was an Irish Catholic. Poor wretch gave up her mistake to a Dutch woman. To purify. A few impurities were overlooked, apparently. Just look at him swill that Canadian.

"I feel much remorse, Charles."

"Well you don't show it. Is that the only bottle in the house?"

"Drink your fill, lad."

And you will.

"Maybe you hide your feelings. I don't know. I've never really understood you."

"My God, don't try. Save your mathematics for business, whatever your business is. I'm a living contradiction. Nobody understands me. I don't understand me. Got the good Lord Himself scratching the scalp."

"I mean, how can you belong to the Church and act the way you do? You don't make sense."

Jones slapped his son's thin shoulder. An ice cube hit the piano keys.

"Of course I don't. Let's get blistered. Let's talk about mountains of the world. The mountains of Denver. I've always craved mountains. Once in 1942 I went to Boulder to see Francis Hamilton. You never knew him. Fine man. One of the few human beings I encountered in the army. He was a janitor of U. of C. Took me out one day, up in the foothills of the Rockies. I stood there, Charles, getting wild as the scenery. After a while I leaned too far forward and fell into a gulch. I was a kid, of course, so I wasn't hurt. Francis laughed 'til he cracked something. He had to sit down. Oh, those mountains. They made me think of the earth and women and fish and the bottle of apple wine Francis had in his Studebaker. Do you understand,

7

Charles? It made me feel like I did the day I took a roll in Buck Creek with my Sunday suit on."

Charles clucked. "I remember. I was scared of you after that."

"You were? Well, it was spring. The ice was just breaking up. I felt I had to take part in the process."

"I see."

"I don't think you do."

"I see better than you think. I've changed, Fielding. I'm a farmer now. I live in the mountains, too."

"I suppose you've become one of those Buddhist vegetarians or Hindu fruit suckers. . . ."

"Hell. Forget I said anything."

"One of those birds that lives on swampscum and fungi."

"You're always so funny. What a funny fellow."

"Have another, son. You've drunk three quarters already."

"That's right. Change the subject."

"Another, Charles?"

"I think I'm getting drunk."

"Wonderful."

Won't be a cheap one, either.

"I shouldn't."

"All right, don't."

"One more. Then I'll stop."

And sneak your way into heaven. Pouring out my life's blood, for my only son. Poor bastard boy. Her son. Why never my son, Charles? Afraid, I guess. Oddity is my commodity.

Charles hung pale on the bathroom door. Fielding Jones took him by the arm, tucked him into his childhood bed and covered him with a cowboy blanket. My baby. Hope

I haven't led you both to the pit. Enough of that. Enough time to contemplate that. Sarah should have found a good Dutch plumber. Drunk his beer in the closet. Dropped his drawers in the dark. No jumping naked on the bed with a trombone. Hahahaha. Poor old Sarah. Stuck with the likes of me. But unstuck now.

Jones sat deep in a Morris chair staring at the last of a quart of Canadian. Sarah's tapestries hung about him. David and Bathsheba were up above the fireplace, meant for him. There was no trust from Sarah after that Miss Horton business. There's one who'll be at the door in two weeks without her underwear. In heat all through the mourning. She's lying in a bathtub right now oozing for me. Ah, Sarah, there was no trust after that. Thought I was innocent. Innocently seduced. Lord, her bottom was white as alabaster. The Lord gives us talents to do with as best we can. I, created a scoundrel, have been a fair success. And now I'm left a little time for improvement. Love, I did your bidding all these twenty-one years. And now I've a few to call my own. I love you. Wife. Bit too clean. Bit too prim. Served God first, then me. Until we locked the door. And shook the sheets.

3

Fielding Jones waited a week, couldn't stand forced idleness, so returned to his classes at College of the Pines. On the campus he found usual things among the pine cones and plumping elms. Students milling, touching as much as the trustees and John Calvin would allow. And more. The ground was swollen, bursting under his feet. Mud ran in paths across cement, excrementitious elements of awakening earth.

> *And love has pitched his tent*
> *In the place of excrement.*

In through the shining Monday halls to Room 123. His desk was untouched. Open on it was the magazine he'd abandoned a week before. He sat down and finished reading an article on Jane Fonda. Life went on. Path to the main office. In his mailbox was a clutter of demands and condolences. He grunted at Miss DeVries, the secretary.

"Welcome back, Dr. Jones. I'm so sorry about your wife." Her smile was embarrassed, sympathetic.

"Thank you, Miss DeVries."

"If there's anything I can do. Typing . . . letters—"

"Thank you, Miss DeVries. I'll let you know."

Remove your dress, Miss DeVries. Down to that young Dutch skin. Frolic with me in the mud. I'm restless as sin today. And me with classes to teach.

Back to 123. Into the oak swivel chair worn thin in the seat. And it was new when I got it. Good Lord. My buttocks as crisp and round as before and the oak worn thin. There's durability for you. And intimations of immortality. Twelve years in a single job. Unthinkable.

In Room 322 they were waiting, as always. They never could be absent all at the same time. No groan greeted his entry as was usual following an absence. They all knew. Respectful sympathy for Dr. Jones and newly departed wife. Cynical thoughts for a man born to teach. I've even forgotten what class it is.

"I'm back," he boomed.

Relieved smiles flickered like lights in hotel windows.

"What class is this?"

A familiarly odious voice from the back of the room said, "231, sir. And we understand."

"You understand 231, Dozema? Incredible."

"We understand why you've forgotten, sir."

A shy hand fluttered by the windows.

"Miss DeJong?"

"I would like to pray, Dr. Jones." She brushed back her thin ratty hair from two obscure eyes. No one treated Jesus more like a husband than she.

"I supposed you would, Miss DeJong. Proceed."

"Thank you. Let us bow our heads."

A wave of irritated grumbles from up front: a healthy sign.

"Christ has taken up his treasure.
From our lives went Mrs. Jones.
To our lives she brought much pleasure.
Now she's freed from mortal bones.

"Dr. Jones, he is still with us,
Teaching us with wit and skill.
Over us there lays a hush
For him who has helped our lives to fill.

"Let us bow our heads in praise then
And thank them both for such a gift,
And pray that together Christ shall raise them
Into heaven's own snowy drifts.

Amen."

An uncomfortable shifting all about the room. She's written me an epitaph. And as fine as anything Julia A. Moore ever conceived.

"Thank you, Miss DeJong. A little poem. Was that Yeats or something of your own?"

"Oh, my own, sir. I wrote it last night."

"Remarkable."

"Thank you, sir."

"Oh, sir! May I add a sentiment to that?"

"Raise your hand, Dozema. If you wish to speak, raise your hand."

"Yes sir. I'm very sorry."

He raised his beefy arm and waved it at Jones. And waved it.

"As I recall, we were about to leap into T. S. Eliot. 'The

13

Love Song of J. Alfred Prufrock.' I enjoy doing this poem. Why do you suppose that is, Miss Batema?"

Soft, delicious Betty Batema. A week hasn't altered the thrust of that sweater. Time destroys a cell at a time. She won't understand the pain of Prufrock.

Without a blush she said, "I believe it occurs in a house of prostitution, sir."

Gasps came from over Miss DeJong's way. "What poem are you speaking of, Dr. Jones?"

" 'The Love Song of J. Alfred Prufrock,' Miss DeJong. Miss Batema believes it occurs in a whorehouse. Would you agree?"

"Certainly not."

"What is your idea?"

"I haven't read the poem, sir."

"Then how can you disagree?"

Miss DeJong sat firm and sure, righteously indignant as the Old Fellow himself. "Poetry, sir, deals with loftier topics than frailties of flesh. It is the refinement of thought, not the degradation of it."

"That's interesting, Miss DeJong. Who else thinks the poem is about a whorehouse?"

Three or four reluctant hands rose, that beefy one still waving.

"Sir, sir—could I add a sentiment?"

"Certainly, Dozema. When I call on you."

"Thank you, sir."

"What's wrong with writing a poem about a whorehouse?" Surly, wolf-limbed Harry Davis aimed an evil eye at Miss DeJong.

Who stared out at the grim earth. Above all this. "I do wish you wouldn't use that word."

"Shakespeare had all kinds of whores in his plays." Davis leaned forward, his voice a little trembly.

14

"That's ridiculous. Shakespeare is the immortal bard."

"Who was Doll Tearsheet then? Falstaff's mother?" Davis was eager, twirling a lovecurl on a finger. Snickers here and there. Life suddenly fun again.

Miss DeJong fidgeted, managed a nasty smile. "Doll Tearsheet was Falstaff's paramour. Your obsession with that word is a good indication of the condition of your soul, Harold Davis."

"Oh, oh. Tut, tut, Miss DeJong. Let us not judge one another."

You musty, fartical Bible-thumper.

"Forgive me, Dr. Jones. I was provoked."

"You mustn't mistake honest debate for personal provocation. Besides, Doll Tearsheet was a whore."

Davis leaned back, yawning his triumph.

"I . . . I find that hard to believe."

"It is true, Miss DeJong."

"Dr. Jones. I'm seriously disillusioned. I'm terribly disappointed."

"Pray, Miss DeJong. You shall recover."

"But Shakespeare never—"

"Ah, but he did."

"May I add a sentiment, sir?"

"All right, Dozema. If you insist."

"I—I, uh—"

"Yes, Dozema?"

"I've forgotten, sir."

"But this poem isn't about a whorehouse." Davis snapped his ballpoint with a fury.

"You see, Miss DeJong. He's not obsessed. Continue, Mr. Davis."

"I don't see how anyone could think it was a whorehouse."

Betty Batema's arm flew up. One breast rose. "Then

15

who are all those women with hairy arms talking of Michelangelo?"

Davis grew gentler. Strange how soft breasts and a smile enhanced an argument. Mention that to the debate coach. "All women have hairy arms. He means it ironically. A naturalistic twist. He's talking about the kind of women who come to my mother's teas. Phony, brainless women. Know what I mean, Dr. Jones?"

"Believe I do, Mr. Davis. Go on."

"I mean these women have got Prufrock there and they're pinning him to the wall. Ripping him up with gossip. He's a writer. Must be about your age, Dr. Jones. But he's got no guts. These women promote his books or something. He can't stand them, but he hasn't got the guts to tell them where to go. They don't know Michelangelo from beans. Know what I mean?"

"Good perceptions, Davis. Nothing in the world duller than us literary folk. And Prufrock says he measures out his life with coffee spoons. Is that frightening? It frightens me to death. For I—as Davis implied—have a bald spot in the middle of my hair."

"It kind of frightens me." A hand in the back row. There was the ugliest face in school—Zondervan of the rhinitis nose.

"Yes, Mr. Zondervan. Explain."

A wild blush swarmed behind a hundred little pus blossoms. "Well—it's emptiness. Life is empty. Every day you wait and nothing happens."

Dear ugly kid. You know, all right.

"Not if you've accepted Christ as your personal saviour!" DeJong sprang to life.

Zondervan shrank back and disappeared behind Dozema's beef.

16

"Miss DeJong. Dammit, save your zeal for the pagans. Speak when called upon. Otherwise, zip it up."

Shocked disbelief. A measurable tremor passed through the room. To err is human. Except with a trustee's daughter. Jones, what have you done? Dared to eat a peach. And still come off Polonius. No Hamlet here. Ah, well, on with it to the death.

"Is that perfectly clear, Miss DeJong?"

Stone silence from that quarter. Silent applause on faces about the room. Applauding on my grave. I'll leap in laughing, which even Hamlet would not do.

> *And silence sounds no worse than cheers*
> *After earth has stopped the ears.*

Or so it's said.

Walking home through damp streets with mist about the house lamps, Jones was filled with a joyful sense of doom. Every end was a new beginning, every death a birth. Autos swept through ponds gathered about sewers. Odors from houses of meats and baking bread. Through the windows he saw men in undershirts leaning into newspapers. Shifting television images flashed out into darkness. The saturated air made a fine film on his skin. As he hunched through the April streets.

On Talbot Street he paused, noticing a light in his kitchen window. He had never needlessly burned a light in his life. Sarah could get up a fine fury about the lights. Felt she needed one on to bathe. She never knew the joy of bathing in the dark. A cent every three hours soon added up, and now someone was draining the current with him not there to utilize it.

19

He neared the door, heart thumping out burglars. Rapists . . .

"Fielding, darling. Your door was unlocked. I've been waiting for hours."

"Good Lord. Miss Horton. It's you."

Miss Horton draped herself in the Morris chair, under David and Bathsheba, looking very much at home in tailored pants and a loose knit sweater, traces of black underwear all about, legs crossed Indian style of liberated, near-forty ladies with faintly wrinkled eyes and too-crisp hair. And I wonder of the precision of that alabaster bottom, what ravages three years have worked.

"I brought you dinner, Fielding, dear. My intentions are purely sympathetic. Poor man. Bereaved and alone. I couldn't bear the thought of you eating, cooking by yourself night after night. I've brought some steak and sausages and a bottle of pink chablis."

"That's decent of you, Miss Horton. I frankly haven't been shopping since the funeral. Sarah took care of those things. There isn't much about."

"Then it isn't indiscreet of me?"

"Sympathetic intentions are rarely indiscreet."

"Good! Then show me your stove and get into something comfortable. Your clothing is damp. Let me hang it up for you. Oh, Fielding, you dear man. Let me take care of you. If only for an evening."

"You flatter me, Miss Horton."

"Please—call me Marjorie."

"All right, Marjorie. I entrust myself to your care. The kitchen is yours. Be with you in a flash."

And up the stairs into the bedroom. Woman's room. Out of this wool suit. Into the shower. No, she might be upon me. One must be dignified in mourning. How long is proper? A year. Lord, I haven't one to waste. Dry the pits. Check the underwear for streaks. Last clean pair in the house. Sarah, where are you? Brush these sturdy teeth with a dash of brandy. Into some soft old corduroy. Not much heft about the middle. Hernia scar from breaking cement. Life's pains writ upon the flesh. And man was made to mourn. But not tonight.

Odors from downstairs. It is fine food and drink. Cooking sounds of Marjorie, filling my house, driving out the cold. And maybe something more than steak and sausages cooking. I'll perish for such thoughts.

In the dining room under the rippled glow of candles, Jones watched Miss Horton touch her upper lip, removing sausage grease. An empty bottle caught pieces of light on the buffet behind her. Another popped its cork, squeezed between Miss Horton's trousered knees.

"My, Fielding. I do feel warm now. We shouldn't open a second bottle. I'm glad you found it, though." A small flurry of giggles, and Miss Horton's cheeks grew flushed as a schoolgirl's.

"Sarah's afterdinner wine. One of her few allowances to bodily appetite. Caught the habit from me, of course."

"Poor Sarah. If only she had not been so inhibited. I shouldn't be talking about her. But a man like you deserved more. Thank God she never knew about our little get-together."

"Oh, she knew, Marjorie."

Bit of a trembling on the surface of Miss Horton's wine.

"What do you mean. She couldn't have."

"She did. God knows how. Maybe He told her. She knew the next day. It was then that she began David and Bathsheba in there. That damned rug has caused me much remorse."

21

"I'm shocked. I feel terrible. I thought she went to the grave without a hint. And that's why you've avoided me all this time. Oh, Fielding, I'm sorry. How can I ever make it up to you?"

There's a loaded question. How to sensibly answer?

"You have made up to me by entering my house this cold evening, Miss Horton. Marjorie. My palate has been delighted. My heart warmed. I could ask for nothing more."

"Except perhaps—"

"Miss Horton."

"I want you, Fielding."

"Miss Horton. I am in mourning. We should wait a decent period—"

"I haven't time to wait, Fielding. Neither do you."

"Miss Horton. Your sweater. Good Lord, I'll get the blinds."

"I want to do things with you, Fielding. Everything you ever imagined. Everything you wanted to do but Sarah wouldn't. Fielding—"

"You do Sarah a disservice, Marjorie. My God, old Velding's staring out his kitchen window. Dropped his newspaper in the dishwater. Marjorie, your pants. Could we adjourn to the den?"

Jones snapped off the overhead, blew furiously at candles. From darkness it's easier to see old Velding and wife pressing noses on a newly steamed pane. Against me, Miss Horton in black underwear undoing my trousers. Father forgive me. Where in hell is the hook? In the front, Miss Horton? Between the melons. Never encountered such a one before. Yes, I remember them, Marjorie. The two I knew in younger days. Nearly as firm, old girl. Trousers hit the floor, coins rolling about the kitchen. Can't get feet out of them. Shuffle into the den where the carpet is thick.

Marjorie has me by the stem. Glands responding despite some worn bearings. Out of one shoe but the pants are caught. Wallet somewhere. More change flying.

Miss Horton leaped atop the desk and hung her panties on Sarah's painting of John the Baptist. I picture Prufrock's head upon a platter. Then my own.

"Ask me. Ask me anything, Fielding. Anything you want."

"Help me out of my pants, Marjorie. They seem to be caught on my shoe."

Hysterical laughter from Miss Horton as she jumps. "My poor Fielding. Give me your foot."

That's not my foot, Miss Horton. Lower. There. A little harder. Ah, you've got it. And let me see you now. Behind. Turn for me . . . a little more. Good! White as a gull's breast. Hardly changed. Something spared me. God, I'm near to tears. This beautiful sight.

"Oh, Fielding. You're so big everywhere. This long lean chest and . . . oh no, you're scarred. That wasn't there before."

"Double hernia. I was cracking cement in—"

"Don't tell me. Let me look at all the length of you. Pull back this skin and peek a moment. Everything's so large, darling. Please tell me what you want."

Softly. That's like poking in my heart. Softly now. My God, how to say it.

"Marjorie."

"Tell me, darling."

"You must promise you won't laugh at what I'm going to ask."

"Never, never. There's nothing you could do that I haven't dreamt already."

"I think there is."

"Name it, darling."

23

"Promise first."

"I promise."

"Would you mind terribly if I played the trombone?"

Miss Horton turning faintly gray. She'd not dreamt that, it was clear.

"A trombone? Whatever would you do with a trombone?"

"I realize this request is unusual, Marjorie. My reasons are rather difficult to explain. You see—"

"You don't mean a slide trombone, do you, Fielding? I don't think that I—"

"No, no, no. Nothing like that. Good heavens. God forbid. What I'm trying to say is that—well—there were a few occasions in my life with Sarah when—"

"Oh, Fielding. You needn't explain."

"Please, Marjorie. I'm getting embarrassed. I must clarify this."

Miss Horton holding me tightly. In a strange spot.

"You see, there were moments in my life with Sarah when I, being more a pagan than herself, desired to . . . dabble in the mysteries and varieties of love. Sarah's fires—how should I say?—were sometimes slow to ignite. Though once fired they proved difficult to quench. Age did not help the situation. What I'm leading to . . . you see . . . well. It was one Sunday afternoon. I was full of juice. You understand. Sarah was full of God. You had to get rid of God before you could even consider the juice. Well, this day God was determined not to leave without a fight. So I had to resort to extreme measures. I went upstairs to our room and stripped naked. I hauled my old slide trombone from out the closet and leaped up on the bed. I played 'Lassus Trombone' with all my might. Jumping up and down. Blew the old guts out. Sarah came running up, horrified that I was howling in the throes of death.

24

But I was very much alive. As she could plainly see. She listened a moment. Then laughed. Then slipped quietly as you please out of her Sunday dress, corset and all, shut the bedroom door on God's nose and locked it tight."

"How exciting."

"It was, Marjorie. And I swear that music worked magic. That long afternoon, yes, yes. The most glorious Sunday of my life."

Jones's ear was suddenly full of Miss Horton's tongue.

"Marjorie?"

"God. Get the trombone. Hurry!"

5

Two choruses of "Washington Post March" seemed to do it. Placing the trombone on his swivel chair, Jones prepared the woodwinds for Miss Horton, her shoulder blades plunging at Sarah's $12.98 a yard Mohawk nylon. Eager movements and forest sounds. God forgive this little prank. Don't breathe a word to Sarah. Miss Horton, are you dying? What do these noises mean?

"Miss Horton!"

"Oh-h-h."

"Marjorie. Are you well?"

"I'm dying."

"Good Lord. I'm hurting you."

"Of pleasure."

"I see. That's a relief."

"I'm not letting you out of here, Fielding."

"You aren't?"

"No."

"But occasionally I like a game of whist."

"Only then. Otherwise your sword shall not leave my scabbard. An ensheathed sword gathers no rust."

"So it's said."

"Every day, Fielding."

"I'm in mourning, Marjorie."

"I'll wait with bottom bared."

"I'm forty-eight, Marjorie."

"Then you must play your trombone."

My little succubus. Should be one in every home. Takes me longer, Marjorie. Wait. Slowly. This ancient easy dance. Sounds in the street distract the soul. Sounds in the driveway. Old Velding's, I pray. Doors clunk. Overshoes on damp cement. Fright piercing the heart. Shriveling the scrotum. Miss Horton moaning like a heated beast. Quiet, dear. Listen to the feet. On the porch. Not old Velding's cement porch. Wooden. I have a wooden. Good Lord, the ghost come back to rattle her rug. Nathan sent to scream his doom.

"You're fading, Fielding."

"I know, Marjorie."

"What happened? I didn't feel—"

"In the closet. Oh my God. Judgment at the door. Un-knot my pants."

A strong hand clouted the back screen. Miss Horton lay scared and pale. On with the robe. Up with the trombone. My hour of practice, which even a death in the family cannot forestall. A blanket in the closet. Room for you among the shoes. Silent prayers, Miss Horton.

Into the kitchen. Pounding around the frontal lobes. Bras, socks, clothing all about. Gathered safe in the oven with the sausages. Change shall have to lie where it is. And a smile to meet the faces that we meet. A turn of the curtain reveals Dean Vredevelt and Clarence DeJong,

College of the Pines' saintliest trustee. A lovely sight. For holier hearts.

"Gentlemen. What a surprise. Please come in. Just practicing my trombone. Seems to help fill the void in my house."

In with the draft come these two worthies.

"Ah, yes, Fielding. I understand. I didn't know you played, though." The Dean's smile was nervous. Something was up. Clarence looked grim as a hard stool.

"Sounded like someone in pain in here."

"Ah, ha, Mr. DeJong. That describes my playing to a tee."

Clarence looked about the room, making little memos. Jones's money on the floor, empty bottle on the buffet, Sarah's bottle on a chair. And—great God—the soiled settings on the table. Half a sausage in a dish. Beside it an earring. Walls are closing in. Organs of evacuation quivering.

"What has happened here? Are we interrupting something?"

"Good heavens, no, Mr. DeJong. I can practice anytime."

"I mean these coins on the floor. Your dinner table . . ."

"Yes . . . well. I'm afraid my nervous habits are cluttering the house. Pitching coins into a cup. Setting a place at table for Sarah. Taking spirituous liquors to assuage my grief. Gentlemen, it is all my grief. Please forgive my oddities. Come into the living room and tell me what is on your minds."

And breathe softly, Miss Horton. Crouching amid the sneakers.

Jones shepherded them into the dim safety of the living room and scrambled to scratch up a fire. DeJong struck a beatific pose before that infamous tapestry. Dean Vredevelt wandered about, feigning interest in Sarah's relics. Fearful as I. Something unpleasant in the air. News from the holy daughter, no doubt.

"Fielding. We've come tonight to settle a problem. I would have preferred it wait until tomorrow, but Mr. De-Jong insisted."

No time for pleasantries. Haven't even offered sardines.

"Well, Dean, I certainly hope it's nothing serious. I'm not sure I'm up to anything heavy so soon."

"I considered that, sir."

"Mr. DeJong?"

"But my conscience compelled me to act on the matter immediately."

"Would you care for a sardine?"

"What? Certainly not."

"Dean?"

"No thanks, Fielding."

"Then you won't mind if I have one. Part of a can here on the mantle. Little dry but very tasty."

Toss down two and breathe on DeJong. Marjorie suffocating in the closet. Got to get them out.

"Now then. Would you care for a glass of mountain rhine? Perfect with fish of any kind. Sardines to spermacetis."

"Mr. Jones. Today my daughter returned from college literally crushed by a profane outburst she claims came from you and some others in your class. I have never had reason to question her word, but I'm giving you the benefit of the doubt this evening. Is this allegation true, sir?"

Ah, yes. What tact would Volpone invent for such a crisis? Blessed be the man with literature on his side.

"I beg your pardon, Mr. DeJong. Would you repeat that? I'm afraid I was thinking of something else."

"Please, Fielding."

"Sorry, Dean. The mind is everywhere but on my business."

Clarence became slightly crimson and puffed about the jaw. "Your problem is not unique, Mr. Jones. I lost my wife not three years ago. Now I'm left to raise a daughter in as proper a way as I can. And it seems that your conduct in class, if I understand my daughter correctly, does not come up to my standards of propriety. What have you to say to that?"

"I would say that your daughter's estimation is probably correct."

DeJong's meaty jaw champed. "You mean you admit to shouting profanity at her?"

"Maybe I do. Maybe I don't."

"Fielding. Answer Mr. DeJong. This is serious." Poor Dean, quivering about like a moth at a light.

"I'm perfectly serious. How do you define profanity, sir?"

DeJong grimaced, needing suddenly to think. Then a smug smile. "Profanity is taking the name of the Lord in vain. I'd hope you'd know that, Mr. Jones. Noted English professor that you are."

"Yes. I simply wondered if your definition agreed with mine."

"Then you admit your guilt."

"Certainly not. I deny it."

Hold on, dear. Sweet white bottom cold in my closet. This may take a bit longer . . .

"You just admitted it!" DeJong's eyes were moist and pulsing. The Dean sank limp into a chair.

"I admitted that my classroom conduct probably did not come up to your standards of propriety."

"And you deny using profanity?"

"I do."

"Sir. My daughter does not lie!" His fat fist crashed on the mantel, upsetting a sardine can.

"Gentlemen, please. I'm sure this matter can be settled without shouting."

"I quite agree, Dean. Sarah and I made a rule never to raise our voices in this home. I would hope that we all could respect that rule even though she is gone."

The Dean nodded. DeJong stooped to retrieve the sardine can, so rudely tipped. Flushed in the face. Sucking wind.

"I—I'm sorry. This matter has upset me."

"Quite right, Mr. DeJong. And with Mr. Jones also upset, I suggest we take up the matter at another time."

"No! It will be settled now or never. My daughter has been hurt and her integrity questioned. I will not leave until I have the truth!"

My God, Marjorie. Please don't die in my closet. Patience, and you'll have me every day, combatting rust to your heart's content.

"The neighbors, Mr. DeJong."

"Hang the neighbors! I want the truth!"

"You have the truth, sir."

"Then my daughter is a liar?"

"I haven't the faintest idea. I don't consort with students. I know she is the weak-eyed girl who sits by the window. I know she has made it her mission to convert all who do not look constantly to the heavens. But as to whether she is a liar? I should think you could judge that better than I. You are her father, after all. Perhaps you aren't spending enough time with her."

"You stop that impertinence. I'll have your job if you aren't careful."

"And what will be the charge?"

"Impertinence, that's what!"

32

"Dean Vredevelt. Is impertinence grounds for dismissal?"

"What? Well . . . no, I don't believe so. It isn't specified in the contract, as I recall. You are a tenure teacher . . ."

"Aha! That is true. I am a tenure teacher. Meaning, Mr. DeJong, that if you wish to pry me from this establishment you'll need to hang a morals rap on me. Or kill me."

Muffled noises from the den. Tone down the morals business. Please, Marjorie. A moment longer and you'll have whatever you want. Seventy-six trombones.

"You shouted profanity at my daughter! That is grounds for something!"

"I did not shout at your daughter, Mr. DeJong. I never shout. You shout."

"You used profanity!"

"I didn't. I said 'Dammit, Miss DeJong, save your zeal for the pagans.' Something like that. She was interrupting discussion and I told her to stop. Your daughter has the uncanny ability to wrench any topic—any topic—into a full-blown sermon. We were discussing T. S. Eliot, not salvation. But I suppose you are responsible for that eccentricity."

"There! You heard it, Vredevelt. He said 'dammit' to my daughter."

"Fielding?"

"I said 'dammit,' Mr. DeJong. That is correct. I did not say 'God dammit.' I would never say 'God dammit.' I said simply 'dammit.' God was never mentioned. Thus, applying your definition, I am guiltless."

"Dammit, Jones! You implied God!"

"I did no such thing. I never imply God."

"Vredevelt! Tell him he implied God."

"What he implied is not the question, Mr. DeJong. We can only deal with the concrete in such cases."

Well said, old Dean. Assert that manhood. And grieve tomorrow.

"All right, Jones. All right. I'll let that one go. But there is more. My poor daughter blushed to tell me. Blushed, Jones!"

"She does that to an inordinate degree. Perhaps you should consult a physician."

"Jones! I warn you."

"Please, gentlemen."

"Forgive me, Dean. I actually like the girl. She's harmless enough. Feels she has a corner on Jesus, but I won't blame her for that. As a matter of fact, she wrote me a poem. An elegy of sorts. I was quite moved by it."

Take that, DeJong, old man. Sugar with the salt. What say now?

"My daughter has always respected you, Jones. I won't deny that. In spite of your rather frivolous attitude. But that only intensified the shock of your obscenity."

"Obscenity?"

"Whores and whorehouses: You know what I'm talking about, Jones. The classroom of a respected church college is hardly the place for such degraded topics."

"Whore is a perfectly respectable word, Mr. DeJong. You'll find it in Webster's *New World*, Shakespeare, the Holy Bible, and a number of less authoritative sources."

"That's a lie."

"Shall I quote you from Revelations? The minor prophets?"

"No! Never mind. I've made my point. My purpose was simply to warn, Mr. Jones. I know you are a popular teacher. But beware of being too free. Do you understand?"

Soften a little for you, DeJong. Miserable Pharisee. For

34

Marjorie dying in my closet. For your palpitating heart, Dean.

"I understand, Mr. DeJong."

"Good. I've made my point. I believe in getting things settled, Dean Vredevelt. We can leave now."

"Excellent, Mr. DeJong. Thank you, Fielding. By the way, do I smell something burning?" **1734124**

"Burning, Dean?"

From the kitchen smoke came billowing. A haze on the ceiling. Good Lord, the oven. Didn't Marjorie shut it off? Old Velding will have the fire department. If the vice squad isn't first.

Jones tore to the kitchen, two unwanted samaritans behind. Into the inferno with tongs. Out with a flaming bra. Marjorie's wool trousers smoldering. Such a stench. Under the faucets. The Dean with her smoking net sweater.

"Good heavens, Fielding. What is this?"

"It's rather hard to explain, Dean. Perhaps I shouldn't try." Open the screen and prop it with a shoe. Old Velding out on his porch. Everything okay. Hahaha. And keep hands off that bloody phone.

"Yes, Jones. What is this? Your actions are odd. Are you in the habit of cooking clothes?"

"Ah, ha. Good wit, Mr. DeJong. Actually, I'm destroying Sarah's clothing. Every reminder brings me grief."

The Dean frowned, doubting my word. "Perhaps you should donate it to our mission store, Fielding."

"Yes. Good idea, Dean. This doesn't seem to do the job. I'll go down first thing in the morning. Good-bye. Good night, now. Drive carefully."

Far away.

To the closet to save my dying Marjorie. Eyes smarting from smoke. Tear open the door. And she is gone. A low laugh from behind. Spreading naked across my desk, Marjorie sipped a Canadian.

"Magnificent man. I heard it all. I nearly ran out to congratulate you."

"I'm pleased you didn't."

"Would you care to continue?"

"I'm not sure. I'm numb."

"Let me touch. Rub the numbness out."

"I've burned up your clothes, Marjorie."

"You did? I wondered what was burning. It's all right. I'm going naked from now on. Oh, Fielding. It was hilarious. If DeJong could only see you now."

Marjorie's eyes flew up and by me.

"Fielding? Are you there? I've forgotten my—oh!"

Behind, in the open door, Dean Vredevelt turned to salt. Blinking madly, his eyes stuck to Marjorie. Jones captured now with trombone lowered. Sin will not go undiscovered. It will out. Doesn't pay. Never quit. Always caught. A lesson there.

"Dean. Yes. Well. Good Lord. I'd like you **to** meet Miss Horton. She's a friend of the family."

The Dean couldn't bend his limbs. His evening was ruined.

From his lips came a dry whisper: "I shan't judge."

"What, Dean?"

"I shan't judge."

"I don't know what to say, Dean."

"I shan't judge, Fielding. I shan't judge."

"I should be deeply ashamed."

"I shan't judge."

"With Sarah just dead."

"Only a week, Fielding."

"I believe I am ashamed."

"I shan't judge."

"Have I lost my job?"

"I—see me tomorrow. Oh, Fielding."

"I know, Dean."

"DeJong is in the car."

"Please keep him there."

"Oh my God, yes. I forgot my muffler. I'm always forgetting my muffler.

"Good night, sir."

"Good night, Fielding."

"Nice meeting you, Dean Vredevelt."

"Yes. Miss Horton."

And out into the cruel night. Dear man. What have I done?

"Good Lord, Marjorie."

"Oh, Fielding. Take me home."

"It's horrible."

"I'm going to cry."

A vale of tears. Mother knew.

6

Jones crouched in the garage, groping for keys to raise the Ford from the dead. Marjorie waited in the shadows with Sarah's housedress on, the one she'd lifted for him so many many times. Up with keys and oily palms. Blood on the hands again. Life seemed a long succession of regrettable moments. At this moment. A soggy moon drained through the window, and Jones belched a sardine.

"Get in, Marjorie. Safer inside than out."

Marjorie crawled into the dust and rust.

"My God, Fielding. Is this your car?"

"Yes. Do you like it?"

"It's horrible. Filthy. Makes my skin crawl."

"Only forty dollars, though. It has new wiper blades."

"It's ugly."

"It suits me."

"What did Sarah think of it?"

"Sarah tolerated it. As she did me."

A few coughs and Casite fumes burst at the back and through the floorboards.

"Open the windows, Marjorie. No, close them. It's worse outside."

"I'm dying. Get me home."

"Be patient. We'll have fresh air through the boards in a moment."

The wagon rattled out of the driveway, old Velding watching at the front door. Jones, saving the brakes, leaped a curb and wheeled into Talbot Street on dead shocks. A blow to the teeth.

"Oh my God. This is a nightmare. Get me home safely, please."

"My apologies for that bump, Marjorie. I think we're dragging something."

A trail of sparks danced behind the car. The shrill lamentation of metal on stone. My God, it's got the hemorrhoids.

"I don't care. Get me home."

"I believe it's the gas tank."

"Get me home."

"But Marjorie—"

"Please, Fielding."

"I wired it on. Must have jolted loose. I'm not sure we should go on—"

"Then stop. I'll walk."

"What is that smell? I'll walk, too, I think. Out quickly. My poor car. And still two good tires on it . . ."

Marjorie stood in the damp without her underwear. Breasts a little low, forlorn. Her heated bottom cold. Sarah's dress hung too long in the hem and too limp in the arms. And all the passion gone. Robbed of our time by some vengeful force.

40

And when the Ford exploded into flames he turned to watch.

"Oh, Fielding. Your car."

"It served me well."

"I'll run home and call for help."

"Thank you, Sarah. Marjorie, I mean. You look like Sarah in that dress. God, what a night. Shall we ever try again?"

"Not for a while, Fielding."

"All right."

"I'll go. People will see us together."

"Does it matter?"

"I suppose not. Good night, Fielding. We never even got to—"

"I know."

Alone in a cold bed, two pillows now his own, Fielding Jones considered the wages of his sins. His forty dollar car was gone. And two good tires. Twenty to tow the husk away. God knows what for fire department services. Or did one pay for those? Sixty dollars anyway. And Marjorie home in gloom, her passion spilled. The Dean, poor man, abed, awake, my sin squatting heavy on his chest. And another moment lost, too valuable to give a price.

Jones, Jones. This stout heart should quake at fiery warnings. Mother would read the signs of doom. St. Elmo's fires cracking in Ahab's eyes were no clearer than these. When doubts arise, Canadian is wise. A few beakers before I dream.

Behind the eyes appear an empty theater, a shabby stage of few lights. Burgundy curtains, stained by cabbages and different sorts of fruits, open in a squeaking, paralytic manner. Jones takes a seat, straw and springs pushing out beneath him. Three figures appear on the left. They sit in dusty shadows of an old Dodge coupé, moving slowly down a gravel and dust road called by some village sage the Divine Highway. In the wake of the Dodge is a large brown cloud that blots out all the scenery behind. These three slowly lose their muted haze, focus, until Jones sees that one of them is himself, the closest one, sitting at a right side window, touching a large, ripe pimple at the corner of his mouth. A boy. Who is hypnotized by fleeting giant trees that bound the road. Beside the boy, silent and staring, shoulders humped, knees up, sits his grandfather Jones; beside him Emerson Jones, the father. Driving with a single finger. Talking endlessly about the virtues of the Ford. The three are jammed up, shoulder to shoulder, in the particle-cluttered air of the front seat.

And the Dodge bungles along like a wormy dog dragging its behind. Through towns they move, small Midwestern towns that are not unlike thousands one might pass on a gravel highway. From his theater seat Jones sees them: Owosso and Pewamo and Ovid and St. Johns, Muir and Lyons and Saugehawk and Saranac; all of another time. All with ugly, square Victorian buildings, stores beneath and dismal windows above. Three gas stations with single pumps. One always a Standard. A paintless wreck of a mill through which a river wanders. It is the Eel River. A John Deere farm equipment store. One dim marquee announcing a movie shown a year before in the cities. A drugstore where the town's young people meet over chocolate fizz and strawberry ices to discuss automobiles or somebody's hired girl. And a farmer's tavern with a "Drink Sebewaing" sign, where dung and straw smear the floor and a village idiot dances in the corner for coins.

44

They pass a Grange Hall. Emerson Jones points and says he played for dances there when he was thirteen and drank hard cider in the back with the men of his band. Jones imagines the soft-eyed boy lifting a jug and laughing in the middle of a cornfield in the middle of the summer in the middle of the night.

He blinks as the car halts. They are in Portland, at the Eel, renting a boat from Ralph who also sells Eel River snapping turtle soup. The grandfather stumbles into the stern as the others steady the bow. Emerson Jones rows. The boy pushes off, rocks and grass sliding beneath him. Sliding away beneath him. The boat creates a flutter in the shallows. Emerson Jones strokes the glass and they shoot out into the current and are caught. The oars are out. And he, dipping them now and again, keeps them straight in the old hulk. Drifting like some moss-bellied sleeping fish. Down, down through cathedrals of trees and sky, down by shadows and sun-dried rocks with turtles diving. And a smallmouth bass wrenching himself into the air and flopping back.

The pull of the stream is irresistible. It frightens them in an odd way. For though Emerson Jones holds the oars, he does not control a hand that grips and pulls them down this surface of the world. Occasionally they catch a rock and pivot to the side as the old wood groans. Jones's heart jumps. He gets to his feet, moving to the edge of the stage.

Then, swinging wide on a bend hung with willows, the grandfather stands and points. "Sit down," says Emerson Jones. The old man does so grumbling, and they look to see what they have journeyed for. Six ancient elms rot in dignity on the grass banks. Behind them dry September corn spreads outward and back. The grandfather's eyes see spirits in the corn. Of eleven brothers and sisters. Grandfather's father sweating in the corn rows. Mother in the house beyond, preparing biscuits and boiled potatoes. Singing quietly to the cat who hangs on every odor. The boy watching his grandfather's eyes. Jones watching the boy's. The current sucks them downward; Emerson Jones fights it but soon the corn is out of sight and the bank and the elms. And the grandfather begins humming "Asleep in the Deep."

Fielding Jones, leaning on the stage, watches the three drift away. There is a bend downstream, a point of land. A very small child sits on the point, fishing with a long cane pole. The child has a Mongoloid head and withered limbs. Jones sees who it is, groans deeply. "Row back!" he cries. Pounding fists on the stage. The three sit quiet, floating lazily toward the outthrust pole. "Row back, for God's sake! Sarah, stop them! Don't you see? We don't want that! Stop!"

Fielding Jones fell from bed into a heap of dirty underwear. Cold with sweat. Heart pounding. Eyes alive. At the open casement window, rain whispered. Taking Sarah's picture from the dresser, he snapped on a light and crawled back into bed.

I've dreamt it again. Dreamt it again. David Emerson Jones, child of my loins. And no Sarah to rub the dreams away. Poor David Jones, whom out of your goodness, Sarah, I caused to come. David of the large head, who only learned to grind his teeth and died. And you enfolded him, Sarah, without shame or malice, and would have found room for any other David I might produce out of this vast imperfection of flesh and spirit. Child robbed of life. Wife of time. And I am left. With poor Charles, our foundling. Sadness rushing in my blood. And no wife to rub it away.

46

Sarah, David, father, grandfather. Forgive me. For it all. For being left. When you are good. But gone.

And Jones sat, waiting for sunrise, watching the huge, gentle arms of elms that dipped low about his darkened, empty house.

8

Morning. To the can to feel flaming start of a kidney infection. Jones opened the bureau where he saved old pills, found a jar of last year's kidney boluses and wolfed down two with some juice of the prune. Nectar of the faithful. Ye olde regulator. Softening even the hardened sinner. Then up on his morning perch with an Agatha Christie mystery. But half an hour brought no luck and a ringed backside. Much music to be faced today all stuffed and fouled like this. The pain of age, clearly. Age was the only disease. Ralph Waldo knew—in his silent senility preferring soft stools to transcendental visions.

The April day was bleak, but Jones looked to the light with relief. He unhung a rusty English bicycle from the rafters of the garage and set off down Talbot Street, briefcase swinging from the bars, muffler flying, pant legs clamped with rubber bands. Into town, dodging in and out lines of cars, past huge smooth buildings and smiling women with shopping bags. Onto campus with sun breaking through the sky, pines suddenly aglow, students hacking into morning cigarettes. Life starting anew.

But the Dean looking very old. Deep in his office chair.

"I've decided to forget about last night, Fielding. What you do at home is your business. Strange as it may be." He was dry in the throat and had dandruff on the collar. His suit looked slept in.

"Dean. I'm grateful. It's unfortunate you had to be a witness to my . . . follies. Miss Horton got a horrible jolt. You quelled her passion. Lord, it's enormous, too. Poor Miss Horton. Please understand her, Dean. All that maiden fire suppressed so many years . . ."

The Dean's lips softened slightly. "And you, Fielding, took pity on her."

"Yes, yes."

"Be glad I'm not DeJong."

"I've thanked God many times for that."

"He'd have you by the neck."

"Or some more private portion of my anatomy."

"I've known you too long. And I know you're good for this college. Unusual as you are."

"The college is good for me, Dean."

"You keep us loose. You temper the DeJong in all of us."

"I do?"

"You do, Fielding."

"I wonder what J. Calvin would say to that?"

The Dean relaxed, thumping an eraser against a grinning tooth. "I'm not sure."

"Good thing he's dead and gone."

"Perhaps it's better."

"In pace requiescat."

"Do you want a leave of absence?"

"A what?"

"The rest of the semester. Go away and settle your mind."

"Do you think I could?"

"Probably not. But the leave is yours if you want it."

"With pay?"

"You're up for sabbatical."

"But I haven't any project going."

"Think of something."

Jones wandered to the open window. The sky was now ablaze with morning sun. "A leave of absence. Yes. I want it. I need it now."

"Some project, Fielding."

"Project. Let me see. Un-m-m. Yes. I've got it. Research into the human soul. A study of the possibilities of life. What say you, Dean?"

"I'll tell them you're going to write a book."

"A book? Yes, I may write a book."

"Then it's settled."

"I'll leave today."

"Next week. Maybe. The forms are ready for you to sign."

And sky's ablaze.

> . . . *Rowing home to haven in sunny Palestine,*
> *With a cargo of ivory*
> *And apes and peacocks* . . .

My heart thumps mightily. I'm off to book a Super Chief to the East. No. To the West. A classic gesture. Journey into dreams of Eden. A weather-beaten Adam, to be sure, who'll hound the sun and howl it down. And not let it sink soundlessly into that Western end of earth.

On the way to classes Jones found a dead pheasant in

the Union parking lot. Stashed it in his overcoat and awarded it to Harry Davis for literary excellence: the Golden Pheasant award. And a feather to Betty Batema on general principle, for her two cradled Cornish hens. The gizzard to Dozema and Miss DeJong. A few soiled tail feathers, too.

And then good-bye to all my babies, whom I liked in spite of themselves. A final look at the antiseptic tiles of the English faculty lounge. A pat to Miss DeVries, causing shock, and farewell to a few colleagues wandering the halls. Jones, good friends, bids adieu. Off to anywhere, but Denver first. To the mountains of the world where first I woke to wonder. And to my orphan boy, Charles the farmer. I'll pitch my tent atop a respectable foothill and soak in mountain streams. Contaminating water supplies and spreading disease. And good cheer, too. And the something I've picked at the edges of all my life I'll grab and devour whole. Gizzard and all. If things go well. And I have time to spare.

9

Miss Horton wept gently into the phone when Jones told her, but wouldn't come to the house for fond farewells.

"We'll wait, Fielding. When you return. Maybe."

"Your tune has changed, Marjorie."

"I know. I'm sorry."

"We haven't much time."

"I know, Fielding. I've wanted you for all these years. And now—I don't know. I'm so ashamed."

"Marjorie—"

"I'll never be able to look Dean Vredevelt in the face again."

"The Dean has forgiven us."

"It doesn't matter. I can't help it."

"Shame is a common human condition. We shouldn't let it disable us."

"That's easy to say. You weren't standing there completely naked."

"And thank goodness. It might have cost him a hemorrhage. Poor old Dean. But I dare say he's seen a naked woman in the light before. Though never such a lovely one. Is your bottom cold, Marjorie?"

"Stop it, Fielding. You'll only make me feel worse."

"It is cold."

"Yes."

"Come over and I'll warm it."

"No."

"I'll come to you."

"We mustn't, darling. Stop."

"I'm off to Denver in the morning."

"Oh, Fielding. For the last time, no."

"I'll bring my trombone . . ."

"Good-bye, darling. I'll be here when you return."

And so the job of packing up alone. These ancient clothes. And pills of all kinds for emergencies of the innards. A tube of pucky for the facial dermatitis, and one for granulated eyelids. Juice for fungus of the ears and Dr. Scholl's for cracking toes. A little sulfur solution for flaking of the cranium, so noticeable on a baldy place. And shut down this empty house, saving some water for a morning coffee. And Fielding Jones was once again abed, contemplating mountains, lying on the remains of an excellent uprightness.

At the C&O depot, 6:45 A.M., a cabbie cursed and staggered with two U.S. army duffels and a trombone case. Jones stalked behind, shouting orders, then tipped him a dime and shook his hand. Onto the Super Chief to Chicago, assisted by a conductor who doubled as ticket taker. Jones kept a hand duffel and gallon thermos of Manhattans at his side.

"Little refreshment?" The conductor, dressed in dirty

gabardines and some headwaiter's soiled jacket, grinned through several teeth.

"Full of tropical fish. I'm an old collector."

"Slip me a sip later on and I won't tell."

"Ah, well. Find a clean dixie cup and we'll drink to the golden spike."

"Gimme an hour, friend. Have to see to the other passengers. If there are any."

Down the length of three passenger cars Jones could see maybe a dozen heads, mostly black. A little heap of orange peelings lay at his feet. The varnished sideboards were cracked and flaking, foam rubber crumbling from an armrest. And forty dollars cheaper than a jet.

"Business off?"

"Off. Two weeks from today and I'm shit out of luck. Last passenger run to Chicago. Ever, I guess. Twenty years at it."

"Bring two dixie cups, friend."

"Yeah. You bet. Nice to have you aboard."

And cold smoke curled in the morning yards. A tired porter loaded baggage. Careful of that case, sir. So much depends on a slide trombone, glazed with brasso. Down the aisle an elderly Negro staggered Jones's way in a Goodwill Industries suit and limp Panama hat. Some kind of fake bird squatted on the brim. Behind him, in a ragged patent leather overcoat and pointed purple shoes, came a strange orange-haired young man with freckles covering his yellow skin and a bottle's neck stretching out his coat pocket. Ears like suitcase handles; a gentle, girlish grin. Up they bumped to Jones's seat and took one across the aisle.

"In there, Mr. Armstrong." The orange one helped his companion in with a casual grip of the arm.

"Thank you, Mr. Paris," he whispered.

"Perhaps we can sleep, Mr. Armstrong."

55

"Chicago isn't next?" whispering again.

"No, not next. You must be patient, Mr. Armstrong. And save your voice for testimony."

"All right, Mr. Paris."

Jones leaned over and tapped the orange one. "Fine day, gentlemen."

The two eyed him suspiciously, Mr. Paris touching his fingertips to Mr. Armstrong's leg.

"You two appear to be traveling men," pointing to the ragged, sticker-plastered satchel at their feet.

No sound from these gentlemen.

"I happen to be the tied-down type myself. Wife died not long ago, though, so I'm taking to the road. I've been to Europe with her. But it's no use traveling with a woman. They're either shopping or looking for a place to eat. You don't meet people. And it costs—my God, it costs. I can have fun for next to nothing. I've never had to spend money to have fun. Not me. The real fun is talking to people like you. I'm Fielding Jones. Pleased to meet you."

Mr. Paris looked to Mr. Armstrong, then back to Mr. Jones. Slowly a hand raised up and Jones grabbed it, a little cold and small with a finger missing in the middle.

"Very pleased to meet. I am Harris Paris from Cairo, Illinois. This gentleman is Mr. Armstrong. Mr. Jack Armstrong, great grandson of Thomas Jefferson by a slave."

"My regards, Mr. Armstrong," taking his limp, veiny hand. "I didn't recognize you."

"Mr. Armstrong can't speak."

"Oh?"

"His voice is extremely weak. He must save it for our work."

"May I ask what you do?"

"If you wish. I am a spiritual physician, Mr. Jones. I have

been blessed with the gift of healing. I cure diseases doctors of the flesh cannot. I have healed Mr. Armstrong."

"You have?"

"Eight times," Mr. Armstrong whispered, holding up as many fingers.

"Please, Mr. Armstrong. I will do the talking. Yes, eight times. He has had cancer eight times, and each time I've healed it with prayer. Thousands have been led to God by Mr. Armstrong's testimony. Thousands, Mr. Jones."

"What's the matter with his voice?"

"Well, fact is I've cured him seven times. Once it didn't take. It was in his throat. We thought we had it, but we haven't given up."

"Amen," in a laryngitic squawk.

"Still a fine track record."

"Thank you, Mr. Jones."

"Say, this may be presumptuous of me, but I've known certain men of the cloth to take a drink when offered. I realize it's rather early, but time is relative when one is traveling. Manhattan, Mr. Paris?"

"Manhattan? Well . . ."

Mr. Armstrong struck him heavily with an elbow.

"Excuse me, Mr. Jones. Mr. Armstrong wishes to speak to me," and turning his back, "listen, you tar face, watch my ribs." Many moments of heated whispering 'til Jones popped the spigot and ears pricked up.

"Uh, well, Mr. Jones. I've always maintained that an occasional libation can be medicinal. Where do we get our cups?"

Jones pointed and Mr. Paris stood, leaving for the men's room. The train startled to life, engines grunting, couplings clanking. One look at my city before I go. Old men watching from the depot windows. No one waving good-

57

bye, until I see Miss Horton reaching out an arm beside her car. Dear Marjorie. I'll play you many a merry tune on my return. She sees and our eyes touch an instant. And we're out of the yards, into woods already, and Marjorie is gone. Skirting the municipal dump, Jones swallowed hard, surveying the smoking remains of humankind. Heaps of iron and ash, graveyard of worldly goods. Kiss the past good-bye.

Mr. Armstrong moaned something. When Jones looked, he was choking in his Panama, the fake bird hanging upside down. Mostly air and a little blood. Heaving 'til his guts pressed up in his throat.

"My Lord. Are you all right, Mr. Armstrong? Can I help you out?"

Mr. Armstrong waved him off, groaning so that people turned to see. Mr. Paris came running up the aisle, face a pale yellow and waving a brown pill bottle.

"Oh, Mr. Armstrong! How remiss of me! We were so troubled getting here we completely forgot."

"Poor Mr. Armstrong. I just looked away a second."

"It comes on him fast. May he have a drink, Mr. Jones? He would enjoy a Manhattan to wash this road apple down."

"What's his trouble?"

"A touch of cancer in the stomach."

"I thought you'd cured him."

"It only half took, I think. We have to keep after it."

"Listen, Mr. Paris, you don't want to give him a Manhattan. You'll kill him."

"He only takes his pills with a fix, Mr. Jones. A small taste of wine or whiskey."

"What's the pill? I thought you just laid hands on him."

"Well, this is a vitamin supplement."

"A vitamin supplement to prayer?"

"Excuse me, Mr. Jones. May I?"

"Take it. Have all you want. Let's all have one. Has he eaten?"

"Not today."

"He can't do that. I have a ring of pickled bologna in my duffel. You take it all."

Mr. Armstrong groaned, flattened his forehead against the window.

"I believe Mr. Armstrong wishes to forgo the pickled bologna, Mr. Jones. I may try just a sliver, though."

"Well, he ought to eat something."

Harris Paris gently took Jack Armstrong's hat. Off to the can and back with it rinsed and smelling of hand soap, the bird ruffled but righted on the brim.

"Pour a bit in here, Mr. Jones. Take your pill, Mr. Armstrong. There's to be much laying on of hands and testifying tonight. Mr. Jones has help for you. Take it slowly now."

Mr. Armstrong swilled the cupful and reached for another.

"Pill's still in my mouth. Gimme little more, Mr. Paris."

Jones poured drinks all around. The conductor eyed him from another car. One for you too, old fellow. Come and join this band of derelicts.

And down he came to have his cups. Plenty for us all. With the world passing by outside and light bursting over that eastern edge. Now and again I glimpse the vast blue stretch of Lake Michigan between the dunes. Little resort towns huddled in pockets of the lake. Feeling I have friends along who love me for my thermos and for this brief moment huddled together.

"Friends, time has come for a song. This is an instrument I've carried since the days of the great war."

"It's a push button harmonica, Mr. Armstrong."

"Play 'Down in the Gravy Lay' for a sick old nigger."

"Please don't use that abusive word, **Mr.** Armstrong. I've warned you before."

"I've got a juice harp in my pocket, Mr. Jones."

"By all means play it."

"Mr. Armstrong accompanies our saxophonist. He is an extraordinary Jew's harpist."

The conductor slid off down the car to a broom closet. And back with a pint of ginger brandy. Mr. Paris donated his William Penn with a grin.

"For the lumbago," he said. "God works on the cancer and paralysis."

The conductor gulped and shouted: "You boys know 'The Orange Blossom Special'? Be pleased if you'd play it. The old lady broke my record one night. Hit it with a monkey wrench. And I ain't heard it since." He tipped out another beaker of his ginger and sat back.

Jones shrugged down some fine three dollar William Penn, bent a few notes to warm his lip, and began. Mr. Armstrong followed with a round, twanging Jew's harp, good as ever heard by me. Elevating the spirits. Mr. Paris hummed, mumbling broken lyrics, tears filling his yellow eyes. And Mr. Armstrong sang on his harp, never touching a tooth, inspiring me to heights of musical splendor.

> *For never was piping so sad*
> *And never was piping so gay.*

Mr. Paris howled at the rising sun, devouring my bologna, splashing his lapels, laying hands on each of us and looking only distantly theological.

"I'm civilized," he muttered vacantly. "I'm a civilized man. I'm traveling to Chicago."

The conductor cursed his wife with gritty fists, hum-

60

ming three tones off somewhere. All a merry company. A band of profligate souls rejoicing in the temporary sanctuary of this snorting Super Chief.

As they went sliding toward Chicago.

Later, with Mr. Armstrong asleep, the conductor told the story of how he lost his true love and married his wife. Jones played a down-tempo "Orange Blossom Special" for the fourth time. The conductor bent his head, cursing the bitch who broke his record. Then a jerk below. Scream of wheels sliding. People waking up, looking around with glazed eyes.

"What the hell." The conductor pulled himself to his feet. "This ain't Chicago. This is Benton Harbor. Maybe somebody laying back there in six pieces on the track. We don't stop here for anything."

Outside, a dozen grim men in felt hats blocked all the exits. Mr. Paris looked suddenly stunned; Jack Armstrong fumbled his Jew's harp into a vest pocket, whispering, "Look, Hambone, they got our ass."

Mr. Paris tumbled over Jones's legs stretched across the aisle, knocking the U.S. Army duffel up the aisle, tubes and bottles crashing everywhere.

"Something wrong, Mr. Paris?"

"Excuse me, Mr. Jones. We've had an unexpected change in our schedule." Mr. Paris down on his knees, repacking Jones's duffel. Mr. Armstrong quivering, hopping about.

"Come on, Hambone. Mr. Jones doesn't mind picking them up."

"You boys on the run or something?" The conductor backed toward the closet with his bottle protected.

"There's been a misunderstanding," Mr. Paris said with dignity. "We're not criminals."

61

And he dived head first out the open window. Purple shoes the last of him seen. There was some yelling from one of the grim faces. Mr. Paris groaned from outside, face all scraped and hanging with cinders. Pulling Mr. Armstrong's old guts through the frame. And then my friends are gone. Limping down the rail bed toward a field of tall grass. All the grims suddenly ahead of them, behind them, swarming from all sides. Harris Paris and Jack Armstrong swerving. Turning. With no way to go.

Mr. Paris threw his hands into the air. Mr. Armstrong shrugged, sat down in the cinders. And they carried him that way back to the train. In front of the dark, unmarked cars, a scene that touches the very marrow of me. Two dear friends, my Manhattans still sloshing in their bellies, flung out over the hoods of cars. Their persons violated, their bottle confiscated. Mr. Armstrong's Jew's harp tossed into a bag of evidence. Mr. Paris looking with poetic anguish toward the heavens, his arms upraised. "God bless you, sir. God bless you, too, sir. There's been a dreadful error. I've never seen this man before."

Mr. Armstrong very calm and contemptuous, pulled upright to answer questions. And shrugging, saying nothing, pretending to be mute, moving his fingers to some exotic hand language.

"Officer, he's saying 'I am an old man and God knows I am innocent.'"

"How can you tell that?"

"I read the signs. As a faith healer I am accustomed to such people."

"Faith healer my elbow. Let's see you cure him."

Mr. Paris nodded and laid hands on Mr. Armstrong's shoulders.

"I can talk," Mr. Armstrong whispered.

The grims shuffled about, baffled. They came in to

search the seats of my car, but I knew nothing. The conductor ran about busy and practical, attempting to look sober but failing. Then my friends were spirited away in the unmarked vehicles. The train heaved to life, and all became as before. Except for a nameless pain residing just above the kidney, the boneless feeling following a gigantic surge of adrenalin. And the question of what they did, these friends of mine. Axed their mothers or debauched children? Or merely lived. And managed to be caught?

10

Chopping through foul clouds, the train grumbled by the oil islands of Gary. Green ponds hung in the earth, and Jones wished for another jug of Manhattans for the besmirched senses and battered soul. Out to the north lay the great tomb-gray lake, and everywhere iron fires shot from stacks.

Jones closed his eyes. Best to sleep through this. Dream of breezes down from mountain snows. Mountain water rushing on the feet. The image of Marjorie's white bottom carried him all the way into the Chicago station, where he shouldered his bags to another train, small and very full of people. He showed the ticket to a conductor who puzzled at the paucity of seats.

"Not a seat left, ace. That's unusual, all right. We drop a bunch in fifty-five miles, though. Have to do the best you can till then, I guess."

"You guess? I paid for a seat all the way to Denver. You find me one or I'll hang on the emergency cord."

"I don't think you'll do that. Emergency hasn't worked for two years now."

"Then I'll sit up beside the engineer. Talk about government subsidies."

"Can't do that. Rules don't allow."

"I'm dying of a kidney disease and you tell me there's not a place to sit."

"If you don't mind resting on the bottom side of a pail, I can get you that. No other way. Unless you wait on the next train. That's six hours from now."

Jones sighed, tossed the duffel down beside the restroom door.

"Get the pail."

"Yes sir."

"And it better be soft."

"Can't guarantee that."

"Just get it, dammit. If I die, I'll haunt your train. I'll have my revenge. Your company shall pay for my discomfiture."

And off he went in the direction of the engine.

Installed on the under rim of a mop pail, Jones spread his ape limbs across the aisle. A lovely young lady stepped over him to get into the girls'. After a moment of eavesdropping on her ablutions, he watched the nymph emerge from her dressing room; she blushed at his large grin. Then she smiled.

And I, who have lost touch with such signs, can't read the meaning. Insult or invitation? Innocence or action? Haven't the energy or will to tell. But a lovely lady, nonetheless.

The sun started down the sky as deep-cut spring fields opened to our eyes and Chicago passed behind like bad clouds. Wind whipped the poplars and flung out the coats of old men on tractors, old men who sowed the unborn seed with metal fingers, gleaming slabs of earth turned up behind. Where Sarah was, with so many others. Emerson Jones, who took the river as mistress when mother failed, was placed in a hole beside her church, miles from water running free. A sorrowful circumstance even a boy could note. She had him where she'd wanted him all along. But wouldn't have this errant son under extremest of circumstances, including holy writ.

Twenty minutes and the lip of the pail had pierced an arse bone and cut circulation to major veins. Jones opened the door of the boys', lowered the seat and ascended the throne. Feet propped on the bucket outside in the aisle, he sighed deeply, wishing he'd remembered Agatha Christie. He found a paper clip on the back of the tank and cleaned his ears. Then shut his eyes. And heard a voice.

"It's terrible."

"Hello? What?"

"It's terrible that you haven't any seat. I've been watching you for fifteen minutes. I hadn't enough courage to say something earlier. But now I insist that you take my seat. I'm not as light as some women, but I don't believe I'll be a great burden to you for the half hour remaining."

It was the nymph, back to pay a call.

"A burden to me? What do you mean?"

"I will sit on your lap, of course. I see no alternative beyond this impractical one you've devised."

"Impractical? Not a soul has disturbed me for two or three minutes."

"Someone undoubtedly will. Besides, it's undignified. You're an embarrassment to a number of people in the car."

"I am? Good Lord. What have they to be embarrassed about? Tell them I'll trade seats with any of the lot if it will spare their feelings. I'll give up my throne without a battle. You wish me to take your seat?

"I do."

"And offer my lap?"

"Yes."

"Isn't that rather familiar of us?"

"Perhaps it is. But I see no practical alternative. I'll always be willing to sacrifice to make another human being more comfortable."

I look closely now at these large green eyes. Long, glistening auburn hair clasped back. A tiny mole above the lips, set in sweet concern for my old bones. A large lovely girl who has tried but failed to hide her breasts in a navy blazer. Who wishes my lap for half an hour, and whom I cannot refuse.

"That's an admirable attitude, miss."

"It is a rule I try to govern my life by."

"I mustn't refuse then. No breaking of rules on my account."

So off the can and up the aisle, following this knightly lady. Not quite believing such odd events, but eager to be led. And lapped. Beside the seat warmed and molded by her young bottom, a huge man sat, looking rather weary with a cardboard suitcase on his lap.

"I'm back, Mr. Herman. I've convinced him to sit with us."

"Pleased to meet you." He flashed a big, sleepy grin at Jones.

"I'm sorry. I forgot to introduce myself. My name is Lily Robertson. This is Mr. Ulcer Herman."

"Pleasure meeting both of you. Fielding Jones is my name. Two last names are said to be an advantage in this world, but I've yet to discover it." Sitting back into cushioned warmth, my bum at last at ease. Taking her down upon my knees. The gentlest smell of body powder and firmness of flesh. All touching me. And a stirring that will have to be suppressed.

"Are you all right, Mr. Jones? Whenever you tire I'll shift my position."

"I won't tire of this position, Miss Robertson. Excuse me for saying this, but I find the experience exhilarating."

There was a grunt from Ulcer Herman.

"I am only doing this for your comfort, Mr. Jones. I don't mean to exhilarate you."

"You are, nonetheless. But I won't dwell upon the subject. I'm no masher, you know. Please slide back into my lap. My knees are sharp as wishbones."

Taking her by the waist, Jones gently moved her into a compromising position. Miss Robertson blushed as her skirt rose to midthigh."

"There. Now isn't that better? You know, Mr. Herman, this young lady is a rare breed."

"She certainly is that."

"Why, I might have died in that restroom and no one would have noticed. Or even cared."

"You were a sight with them big feet sticking out the door."

"I was? Well, good. A regular conversation piece, eh?"

"I didn't think it was funny, Mr. Herman. Poor Mr. Jones having to sit in a rest room when he paid full fare. It's outrageous."

"Indeed it is." Jones lifted a large forefinger.

"Miss Robertson is a rare bird."

"A pearl of great price."

"Please, Mr. Jones . . ."

"No, I mean it, Miss Robertson. Mr. Herman, your Christian name is unique. How did you come by it?"

Mr. Herman exhaled through big, cashew-colored teeth. "My old mother did it. She had a book of diseases she thought were pretty. My brother was named the same way. Venereal, he fixes tires in Chicago."

"Venereal Herman? That's unique. What do you think, Miss Robertson?"

"I think you're making fun of me."

"I'm not. I'm not making fun. Venereal Herman. Ulcer Herman. That's the truth.

"Kidney Stones Jones should have been mine. I like your mother's idea."

"I never cared for my name. But my mother was good to me. I never would hurt her by changing it."

Miss Robertson shifted, trying to yank down the hem of her skirt. But there wasn't enough skirt there to yank. Lots of thighs and shadowed spots, where I would care to see but won't, for the feelings of this honest lady.

"Mr. Herman and I were discussing birth control, Mr. Jones. Perhaps you have some opinions on the subject."

"You don't say."

"I'm director of a birth control clinic in Chicago. I'm on my way to our national conference in Des Moines. Opinions from laymen are important to me."

"Laymen?"

"Yes. I call them that. I am speaking of the uninformed public. I was trying to convince Mr. Herman that birth control is not a plot for black genocide. It is true we distribute contraceptives in many black neighborhoods. But just as many white women receive our advice and services. Those who believe we mean to diminish the numbers of the black race are simply selfish. The world is at stake here, not black power. We are populating the world beyond its limits of sustaining life."

"Copulating into oblivion."

70

"You might put it that way, Mr. Jones."

That grunt again.

"It isn't a laughing matter."

"I'm not laughing at you, Miss Robertson. Mr. Jones tickles me."

"Well, I want you to believe what I say about that mistaken idea."

Ulcer Herman shrugged, rolled his eyes upward. "I'm not arguing." And in a whisper to Jones: "I got eight kids."

"You don't say."

"Are you speaking to me?"

"You have an interesting vocation, Miss Robertson. Do you walk around with a basketful and pass them out? With the Good Humor men and paper boys?"

"Of course. We both distribute and explain their use. Some women haven't the faintest idea what they are."

"And demonstrations?"

Miss Robertson reddened to a light rhubarb. "Certainly not. We have diagrams. That isn't funny at all."

"I didn't mean it to be. Honestly. What do you think, Mr. Herman? It takes a special kind of courage to walk about handing out contraceptives. I'd be tempted to distribute by airlift."

Ulcer scratched a pink wart on the back of his hand. "You do that, Miss Robertson?"

"Is that strange?"

"Well . . . I'm not saying. Strange to me isn't strange to you."

"Amen, amen." Jones gave her a little pat on the hip. All this bundled flesh, so very large but very nice. Pressed upon my own through several skins of cotton, wool, and something silk, I'd guess. Many serious ladies are serious women underneath. I'd hazard silk for this one. Silk and soft sinful thoughts beneath. "You are a rare creature, Miss

71

Robertson. I hope we shall have time to know one another better."

"Mr. Herman will be getting off in a few minutes."

"I'm sorry to hear that. I don't suppose you'll want to continue on my lap."

"It won't be necessary."

"May I continue here beside you?"

"You may if you choose."

"Thank you, Miss Robertson. I would like that very much."

Mr. Herman mumbled something low.

Miss Robertson's eyebrows twitched. "I beg your pardon, Mr. Herman?"

"I wouldn't use one. Isn't anything more troublesome."

"Is that true? Tell me. This is information I need."

"Oh, true it is, Miss Robertson. They are insidious little killers of passion. They subdue the ancient throb. They're—"

"—like taking a bath with your argyles on."

"Colorfully put, Mr. Herman."

"Why, I'm shocked. I'm very shocked."

"Have you never asked a man?"

"Certainly not. We only distribute to women."

"Miss Robertson, what are women going to do with them things?"

"Why—"

"Miss Robertson, they are terrible, greasy little plasticized—"

"But for the sake of humanity—"

"One rarely thinks of humanity at such moments."

"One must, though. In thirty years the earth will be—"

"In the throes of starvation because we didn't use our rubbers?"

"Yes."

72

"You believe that?"

"I sincerely do."

"That pleasure revoked, too. When so few are granted in the first place. Dammit, we pay enough for our little moments. Forgive me, Miss Robertson. I can't help feeling we're the victims of somebody's dirty tricks. And this could be the dirtiest of all. What else is left when that is gone?"

"It needn't be eliminated, Mr. Jones. Only controlled."

"I refuse to control myself!"

"That's a very poor attitude."

"That I shall cling to. Religiously."

"I feel sorry for you, Mr. Jones."

"Please stop that condescending tone. You're young enough to be my daughter."

"And you're old enough to know better. Your ideas are archaic."

"What is archaic about liking to rut?"

"Oh! Really. You are making me regret my concern for you."

"I'm getting off this train. Excuse me, Miss Robertson. My woman is waiting out there for me. You two better get a suitcase between you."

Mr. Herman rose with his cardboard case and slid by them, Miss Robertson lifting her knees to let him pass. Exposing stocking tops and things that make me gasp. While I'm fighting cybernetics.

"Good-bye, Mr. Herman," she said. "Remember the smaller the family the better the world."

"Yes'm. Whatever you say."

And through the window, which Miss Robertson has moved beside, we watch his brood of eight descend on him like an orphan force, Mr. Herman passing little wrapped candies and rubbing woolly heads, squeezing his enormous wife whose gold tooth catches sun with a burst. It is a warm scene even Miss Robertson seems affected by.

"I'm embarrassed, Mr. Jones."

"You needn't be."

"Big families are beautiful. I won't deny it, though I'm not from one myself. It is very sad to be living now that such a thing has become a threat. I don't think you realize how desperate the situation is."

"Perhaps I don't, Miss Robertson. Or don't wish to."

"Please call me Lily."

Looking at her face now instead of the back of her head. There is a little love mole on her lip and a small downy feminine moustache. Your liquid green eyes, Lily, take my breath away.

"I shall, Lily. My apologies, too. You may call me Fielding. Or butterguts, whichever suits."

And the first smile appears.

"I believe I prefer Fielding."

"In intimate moments my wife would call me the damndest names. And butterguts was the damndest of all."

"You're married?"

"Well . . . yes. In a sense. My wife died just two weeks ago."

"Oh, you poor man. Oh no. Here I am troubling you with problems. My problems. I'm so sorry, Fielding."

"Don't apologize, Lily. Your company is the most refreshing I've encountered in months. Don't let my brashness send you tramping off to find another seat. Please sit with me and talk. I hate to be alone."

"Of course, Fielding. I won't move from this seat. I promise you. Poor man. I hate to be alone, too."

"Ah, Lily."

"Yes, Fielding?"

74

"You are a very serious woman."

"I know. I have to be."

"And very attractive."

The sweet face dipped in a blush.

"I mean it. Serious, attractive, very kind. Are you tied to someone in particular?"

"Only my work."

"Well. That's us pretty much in the same scow. Work can be fulfilling, but it can't be the entire man. I have been lodged in the same job for a dozen years. Have you any idea how long that is? How many years have you been at your business?"

"Three and a half."

"Well, after twelve years passing out contraceptives, you'll know what I mean. Anything can get to you in a dozen years. Including the service of God. Consider how boring perfection must get. What irritating consistency. I'm escaping my profession for a while. Now that Sarah is gone and my adopted son in Denver farming, I am following whither my spirit leadeth."

"How lucky, Fielding."

"I think so. Though it's a bit early to tell."

"What is your job?"

"I teach. I am one of an ancient profession which one pursues when other things fail and dreams die."

"I can't believe that."

"You can't?"

"Some of the greatest men I've met have been teachers. The most exciting moments of my life have been inspired by the words of great teachers."

"Really? Well, I suppose I understand that. Life passed through the fire of thought, tongues of flame—all that sort of Emersonian business. I've had one or two great teachers myself. Made you tingle to listen. I'm stale, though. I feel it. I'm repeating myself. I fell asleep reading aloud to a class one day. There's more to life than that. Something more to put these big fists around before I go Sarah's route. How old are you, Lily?"

"Twenty-five."

"I'm forty-eight. You're so smooth, so large and healthy. You make me envious, Lily."

"I know I'm large."

"Ah, but pleasantly so. Perfectly so. Look at me. All this exaggerated length. A real Cro-Magnon type."

"Your size is appealing."

"It is? You say very nice things. Your size—well, I've always preferred my women with some meat."

"I have that."

"Are you embarrassed by it?"

"Sometimes. When men are shorter and lighter than I. I always feel I should be opening doors and removing coats."

"But you've met your match in me."

"Yes. I know."

"I like you. You're an interesting and honest woman."

"I like you too, Fielding."

"And I see this will be a pleasant journey. I'll buy you lunch."

"You needn't do that."

"But I will, Lily. For being here to talk to. And being good to me. Please."

And taking her hand, Jones led her through hard-boiled eggshells and peanut husks, up to the dining car which wasn't the Ritz. But seeing only Lily's flushed cheeks and green green eyes, accommodations and salty ham make no difference. And there is the light of her splendid smile. Lily, so large, so young. If I touch your hand you won't mind? Though I am twice your age and half your looks.

76

Your blazer off now and breasts revealed, cradled in softest wool. And such breasts they are. Thighs tight in that small skirt. All of you mine a little while. And at least part of me feeling twenty-five again.

"Des Moines is not so far from here, is it, Lily?"

"I'm afraid not. A few hours, I guess."

"A few hours."

"I know."

"It's a damned shame. I've never met anyone quite like you, Lily."

"Nor I like you."

"Maybe it's my age. And all the people gone from my life. I'm reluctant to give up a friend. Especially one so pleasant as you."

"Must you give me up so soon?"

"What do you mean?"

"I feel very forward suggesting this."

"Say it, Lily."

"Have you a timetable to keep?"

"Only in terms of years."

"No one is expecting you?"

"No one knows where I am or what I am up to."

"Then why don't you stop at Des Moines with me? I know this is very brash. I so rarely act on what I feel—"

"You wouldn't mind, Lily?"

"Oh, Fielding, I would be honored."

"A young woman honored by my presence. That's plain madness. But I shall kiss your hand for it, dear Lily."

"You may, Fielding. Before I stop to think."

"I won't give you a moment to think. Thinking is a curse. Take it from me, when you feel joy, grasp it. Grasp it by the forelock. My mother, God bless her soul—and I don't mean to imply she is dead for she isn't, though others who prized their lives are—my mother, in her life, has ac-

77

knowledged no more than three or four occasions of joy. Believe me, Lily. Three or four. That's it. Life is not made for happiness, you know. You must go to church and wait and pray, and pray that you're humble enough to pray. And if there is a moment of pleasure, you must doubt it with all your being. She may be right about the nature of existence, but I refuse to accept it, right or wrong. Life is a vale of tears I'll enter laughing. And leave by the same door. I've stayed with the church all my life. But I won't buy the gloom. I just won't."

"I have experienced some pleasures."

"I don't doubt that."

"But there are so many I haven't."

"Well, I may have missed a few along the way. No matter. Most I've paid for in one way or another. Pleasure is rarely pure for me. There's always some damned catastrophe or other accompanying it. But I won't quit, Lily."

"We mustn't ever quit. That is also a rule of my life."

"And you have a fine set of rules."

"I must work when we get to Des Moines, though. That comes first. I am chairing a discussion group, you see."

"Of course, of course. Work must be first. My pleasure is my work right now. But I'll respect your rules."

"But there will be free time—"

"Which we shall fill to capacity."

Lily, suddenly quiet, watched swift trees passing outside.

"What is it, Lily?"

"I don't know now. I'm feeling guilty."

"How would you feel if I continued on my way to Denver?"

"Very sad, I think."

"But your guilt is worse."

"No."

78

"Well, then?"

"Oh, please come with me. No matter what I say."

"That's it. Trust me. I'll be very kind. You'll soon learn there's nothing to be wary of in me."

Lily smiled, touching a napkin to her lips. Swimming in those large eyes, I see that she is satisfied with my plea. Mustn't act the father's role, though, or she'll be believing it. I am a child of the earth, Lily. Age cannot be measured in years, nor youth in the hairs on one's head. All is relative to the soul's hunger, and mine is crouched and waiting like some sleek animal jungle-born.

"You are so large, Fielding. Maybe you do frighten me a little."

"But I'm very nice."

"And you should be in mourning."

"We get our share of mourning, no matter what."

"Did you love your wife?"

"I did. In a rather halting and imperfect way. Yes, I did."

"And you don't feel wrong going with me?"

"Wrong? What could be wrong? You are a large, lovely young woman. I am an unattached old derelict seeking to fill a void. If we see a zoo or take a stroll together who will care? Feel keenly your own insignificance, Lily, and you'll never worry about the eyes of others. As for God, I think He could find nothing wrong with our compassion. I will do unto you only what I would have you do unto me. Unfair as that may seem to your virtue."

"You preach a convincing sermon."

"Right. It's the pedant in me. We pedagogical types love to hear the melody of our own yap."

"Then we'll go, Fielding."

And we do, into the glamor of downtown Des Moines. Cases, trombones, duffels stacked in the back of a Yellow cab, Lily in a large floppy orange hat which she fears will

79

be crushed under bags of pills. Jones feeling giddy, contemplating a lump on the cabbie's head. And the press of Lily's arm upon his own. With freedom and anonymity to do deeds as yet undone. This Lily Robertson and I. Our fearsome largeness united, an imposing fleshy front against all threat to life.

11

The lobby of the Rudolph seethed with plush, tor-toise-eyed ladies, serious women of all sorts who loved a snap at the officious, slippery-looking clerk. Jones set his duffel in a chair and approached the desk, Lily on his arm.

"Conventions are bad enough. But six hundred ball cut-ters under one roof. Hello, sport." The clerk wiped his neck with a handkerchief.

"Hello."

"I usually smile, but I couldn't iron on a grin right now."

"This young lady has a reservation. Her name is Lily Robertson. Single room for two nights."

"Robertson? Yeah, okay. Room 615, Miss Robertson. Bellboy will be with you in a second."

"And I'd like a single for two nights."

"Sorry, sport. We're booked solid. Two conventions in town this weekend. You'll be lucky to find something downtown. Except a flophouse or two. Try a motel out in the sticks someplace. Howie Johnson or something."

"I'll take anything, a broom closet."

"Wish I could help you. I'd shove one of those harpies out a window if I could."

"What will we do, Fielding? I never dreamed we wouldn't find a place."

"Rule two, Lily. Never desert the ship. If there's an empty room in this town tonight, I'll find it. If not, I'll sleep standing up like the Comanches."

"Fielding, didn't you put your duffel on that chair?"

"Right there, Lily."

Where now a large, crushed velvet tent was pitched.

"Excuse me, madam. Did you move my duffel?"

"I beg your pardon."

"My duffel was in this chair. What have you done with it?"

"Good heavens. Do you think I've taken it? Search me if you wish."

Could be hidden in the folds someplace. Heard of women carrying out typewriters between the legs.

"I'm not accusing you of anything. My duffel was here a moment ago. Now it's not."

"I haven't the faintest idea where your duffel is."

"Lord, it's stolen."

"Oh, Fielding. This is terrible."

"Enough remedies to keep a man healthy for the next ten years. My pajamas, too."

"What are we going to do?"

"You get settled. I'll call the cops. I'll be dead by tomorrow, Lily. Can't live without that bag."

And off to the desk phone to report. The clerk swiped globules from his forehead, apologizing that such things could happen at the Rudolph. Then over to a leather

82

couch to await the constable. A large picture of Pocahontas gathering herbs hung above the entranceway where black men stood in their suits, poised for cars and cases.

And Jones sat, paying for folly already, before he'd even begun. An hour passed. Lily returned, then left to take a shower. Finally, an officer of the law wandered in, scratching his thigh with a clipboard.

"Who lost a suitcase around here?" his voice pounding off the vaulted ceiling.

"Here, officer. I'm your man. Someone stole my duffel."

"What's your name?"

"Fielding Jones. Eel River, Michigan."

"What was in your duffel?"

"Pills, salves, creams, ointments, elixirs, decongestants, ear oil—and a pair of pajamas."

He stretched his thick jaw and settled it back into a pocket of his neck. "You sell pharmaceuticals?"

"No. It's my age. I'll be dead if I don't get that bag back."

"We'll do our best."

"I have a trick kidney. Have to feed it a bolus now and again or it acts up, God help me."

"That's a coincidence."

"You understand?"

"My wife thinks I keep catching the clap. Women don't realize what sitting in a hot cruiser all day can do to a man."

"Ah, bitter truth. You know, officer, once when I was in France, outside Marseilles, I had to put my wife in a café and go out in the woods. Just sat there all naked on a pine stump for a good hour. A healthy pud is a joy forever."

"That's it, all right."

"Get my duffel back and I'll give you some of my pills. I bought a big bottle back a few years ago so I wouldn't have to pay a doctor to tell me what I already knew. Whenever I feel it coming on, I shoot a few down the old tubes and sit up with a bottle of Canadian Club."

"We'll get it back, Mr. Jones."

"Thank you, officer. You can contact me through Miss Lily Robertson, Room 615. At the moment I'm without a room."

And as he left, Lily returned, scrubbed red and clean, dimpled and succulent in a short leather skirt. Would he care to shower in her room, she asked. Replying with violent leaps of nerve ends. Coursing back, memories of the university and bobbing fruits of a nameless Jewish girl asking me to shower in her apartment, whose offer I accepted, terrified at her intent. As I shivered under luke-warm drizzle. Upon me within seconds, tips raised, hands hot, rolling on her painted toes 'til the water boiled. But not so with this Lily of the Lake. Best refuse and avoid the issue now.

On the streets of romantic Des Moines hundreds of sky-larking Shriners strutted in silks and fezzes, in various stages of hilarity and compromise. And as prospects of a vacant room grew dim, Lily's spirits sank visibly, a dimness in the quick of the eye. Jones hustled her into The Blue Goose for a lift of the soul and restoration of the cheek's flush.

She sat sadly, touching brandy to her lips, beneath wild geese flying on a plaster wall.

"It's all my fault, Fielding. I've pulled you off your train and caused you nothing but trouble. I feel terrible."

Jones took up her hand and kissed the third knuckle.

"Dear Lily."

"What, Fielding?"

"Would you have showered with me?"

"I beg your pardon?"

84

"If I had showered in your room would you have soaped my chest?"

And now drinking in earnest: "Fielding. Please."

"Have another, Lil."

"Why are you talking like that?"

"Your offer was the catalyst of the damndest fantasies. I can't lie to you, Lily."

"I wish you would."

"Your leather skirt is very short."

"Is it? I'm sorry."

"Your legs are very long."

"Honestly, Fielding."

"My God, Lily, all that time you spent on my lap has distracted me. There is a simple answer to our problems. It occurred to me immediately, but I've waited to say it."

"Get me another brandy, please."

"Dare I be frank with you?"

"I don't know, Fielding. You weren't like this on the train."

"I was but you didn't notice."

"I'm frightened."

"Of me? Lily, you needn't be frightened of me. I'm frightened enough. Feel this pulse. It triples when I look at you."

"I don't know what to say, Fielding."

"Say you understand what I'm hinting at. Say you agree with me."

There's a trembling in the large pale fingers she's laid upon the table. "My room?"

"That's it, Lily. What say you?"

"My bed?"

"Your bed, your shower, your floor if you wish."

And with boldness out of him, Jones slumped in his chair.

A tear splashed in her empty brandy glass.

"Lily?"

Her eyes had gone stormy as Irish sky. "You weren't like this on the train."

"My God, what have I said? Don't cry. Waiter, a brandy!"

"You aren't the same."

"I know it. Something possessed me. Forget what I said. I'll knock a Shriner on his fez to get a room. Please don't cry, Lily."

"You needn't shout."

"Oh, God. Oh, God."

"Lower your voice, Fielding. Everyone is watching."

"I'm not a lecher."

"I'm leaving, Fielding. Until you quiet down."

"Wait! Sit down. I'll be quiet."

She settled her bottom into the booth, saying nothing. Jones, chewing tongue, waited impatiently. Above him a lethargic fly bungled down a fluorescent light string, singing in small bursts and dim in all hundred eyes.

"You may share my room on one condition."

"I'm not a lecher."

Lily took a Kleenex from her purse and blew her nose.

"What was that, Lily?"

"You must promise not to touch me once the door is locked behind. I'll set out sofa cushions for you to sleep on. Since I invited you to stay on here, I must at least be sure you have a room."

"I mustn't do it. Though I'll be nice as pie. It must be my sickness made me talk like that."

"You're a man. I'm a woman. It's understandable."

"It is?"

"And you are attractive, Fielding. Excuse my tears. I occasionally cry for no reason at all."

"So do I. I could cry right now."

"I've upset you."

"You've upset *me*? I've upset you."

"Please forgive that. Such feelings are only human. Fortunately we're mature enough to overcome them," lifting the glass to her lips, one breast rising in its cup. Simple thrust and fall of a mammary. And the Canadian boils in my blood, killing germs.

"Yes, Lily. Right, Lily. Dirty thoughts are now and forever gone from my mind."

"It'll be fun. I'm glad we don't have to separate. I'll make the room comfortable for you, Fielding. I'm very excited, to tell the truth."

"I'm trembling. My gall has overwhelmed me."

"Come on. Let's walk somewhere. We've nothing to worry us now. I want to find a garden with crocuses blooming."

"First I'm off to find a potty."

And after he's propped against the wall, it's clear the last bolus has worked its little life and gone.

12

Walking with Lily at his side, Jones spoke of Sarah and of Charles, his surrogate son, and, forgetting afflictions, he followed her into a city woods bordered by several sleazy streams. Long shadows of sycamores and oaks cut eastward across the lawns and up the fronts of stone buildings.

"There was a time," Lily pulled up close to his arm, "when I did not question that, no matter what else went wrong in my life, there would always be a blue sky to cheer me. But nothing earthly is absolute anymore."

"There's a cheerful thought."

"Just look at that stream, Fielding. The water goes first and then the air. And last of all, the killer dies by his own gun."

"Christ, Lil. Let's find a crocus and sit in the grass awhile."

"Don't shut your eyes to it, Fielding. That's what everyone does. That's the problem."

"I see it. Thus, I'm a Calvinist."

"And that's no answer. It's simply shuffling responsibilities off on God. Don't you love the earth, Fielding? Sometimes life is so dear to me I want to cry."

"I am a very poor Calvinist in some respects."

"I know. I can tell you're much like me. Did I tell you my father is a rich man?"

"That's interesting."

"He owns a chemical company."

"Truth? Medicines, you mean? Marry me, Lil."

"At last count he had five cars, a yacht, a jet plane, and two homes which usually stand empty because most of his family refuse to have anything to do with him. Mother and I in particular."

"That doesn't sound like you. Harboring grudges—bad business."

"He's a dangerous, immoral man. He is destroying Lake Huron, and he won't do a thing about it. Money makes him that way. Poor father. He's so terribly selfish and wasteful."

"As we all are in our way."

"Don't defend him, please."

"Lil, would you excuse me?"

"Where are you going?"

"Into the forest primeval."

"Can I help?"

"No. Personal business again. Keep off the hounds and the law for a few moments."

Across the grass to the densest sycamore grove in sight, bemoaning age and all its benefits, Jones jogged. Tears welled in his eyes from winds and pains below. Somewhere in a tree a bluejay screamed, echoing a voice within. In a huckleberry thicket he found an unoccupied stump with only tufts of moss and a few fungus fans. Which he placed himself upon, drawers at his ankles, buttocks cold and lightly brushed with fairy dust, to wait out the bleeding of the pump.

Fifteen minutes passed. Twigs and voices came faintly through the sycamores. Jones rose, grasping for trouser tops, but instead tearing his belt from its loops.

"And this, girls, is the *vaccinium ovatum,* better known as the wild huckle—"

A pack of stricken scouts gazed on forest secrets rarely seen. Jones struggled with his shorts which hung immovable at midcalf.

"I—I'm sick."

Their leader, a heavy, masculine type wearing men's trousers, tie and safety shoes, pushed her little band away from the wild huckleberry, a deadly challenge flashing in her eyes.

"Sick, all right. Run, girls. Find an officer. I'll hold him off till you return."

But little looks remained. Until the evil eye turned and dissolved them.

"Good lady, remember the sacred oath of the Brownies."

"Okay, Johnny Weissmuller. I've dealt with your kind before. Exposing your nasty big thing to little girls."

"Good Lord, woman, stay away from me. I was simply relieving myself. I'm sick."

"I know your kind of sickness. Get ready, mister." And through the bush she roared, head down, fists up. Jones panicked, tumbling backward over the stump, catching her ankles with his own. Looking up, he saw safety shoes and thrashing limbs in the midst of a shattered thicket.

With a small secular prayer, he struggled out of the sycamores, fumbling with belts and buttons and zippers. Spotted the Brownies in a giggling bunch on the opposite end of the woods. They hadn't gone for the law. Yet.

Walking as casually as fright would allow, he reached Lily. Dear Lily, who doesn't know what she's taken up with, lying on her back admiring leaves and flying cumuli.

"Lily. We've got to go."

"What is it, Fielding?"

"I can't explain now. I've just had the most extraordinary experience."

"Are you in trouble?"

"I think I am. Could we go to the room now?"

"All right, Fielding. But what could happen in an empty woods?"

"You don't know me."

But someone does. Move by move.

13

Out to the west the shops and houses ceased, cement continuing in solid strips over horizons to the seas, and the great flat plains spread out before him, a hundred miles of treeless, hill-less earth in each direction. Silent F. Jones propped his feet on the radiator and picked at a barbecued rib they'd had sent up. Considering the misfortunes of his life, he groaned and threw the rib into the bag.

"Too greasy?"

"No, it's fine."

"You're angry because I laughed."

"I'm not angry. Just disturbed at my usual bad luck. Misfortune tails me like a heated bitch. Just wait. Someone will bust in here before long and have me for indecent exposure. Or aggravated assault."

"No one saw you come in here, Fielding. Stop worrying. Nothing will happen to spoil this."

She reached, touching his arm with large, delicate fingertips, sparking immodest desires and thoughts.

"I wish I had your youthful optimism. Wonder if they've recovered my duffel yet."

"Dear Fielding. Please cheer up."

"I'm down. Really down. And not even a pair of pajamas to stretch out in."

"Come sit by me a moment on the bed."

"It's no use, Lily. You're best washing your hands of me right now. Before I drag you in."

"Sit by me, Fielding."

So pushing out of the plastic chair, he slumped beside this large-eyed Lily, who gently took an arm and moved a breast against his elbow. That heartbreaking, psoriatic right elbow, which has flaked for forty years. Wagonloads of dead flesh once named Jones.

"Can I tell you something, Fielding. I've never slept in a room with a man before."

Looking into your eyes, Lily, I see the words are honest and pure. But wasted on this luckless debauchee.

"I'm so happy I dared do it."

"I'll be no threat to your purity, Lil."

"Please, Fielding. Hold me a minute. Be cheerful again."

"All right. If you think it will help."

And around her big back he reached, clutching a muscle beneath her arm. Powerful woman, pressing close into me. Heady with smells of clean flesh and hair. All breathing, alive, wondrous. A pimple in your eyebrow I haven't seen before. Sarah pinched blackheads from my brow after we'd loved, searching the scalp with thumbs and nails. Intimate ablutions gone for good, that seem so dear in this distant place. And now someone new, all electricity and nerve ends, hands about my neck and eyes aflood with green. Lord, there's lots of you and all so firm. Lips are licked, I see, and slightly parted. Tongue waiting just behind for my part in the ancient ritual which I have promised to prevent.

"Lily . . ."

"Please kiss me."

"Your resolution."

"Will take effect soon enough. I've wanted to hold you since I saw you on the train. Haven't you wanted to hold me?"

"I'm entertaining dirty thoughts."

"Just a kiss. Please."

And before I can reply the neck is secured in her half-nelson and lips against her own, first dry, then moist. Arms as strong as a Faulknerian bear. But a long, tight, uneducated kiss. All that dedication to the act and she's never learned step one.

"Lil, you kiss like a freight train. Ease off a bit. Here, I'll show you how."

"I don't kiss well?"

"About a C—."

"That's a fine thing to tell me."

"I don't mean to be insulting. I didn't learn myself 'til a priest's daughter showed me."

"A priest's daughter?"

"All in good fun, of course. A friend of the family. Relax your lips, Lily. Too tense, too tense. Open the mouth a little. That's it." What kind of a tongue in your head? Stick it out, girl. Lord, long as a licorice stick. You'll make a champion kisser. Try it once. Lips loose and moist. Move them about on mine. Mouth open. Not too wide. And the tongue does the rest. The tongue is the key. Yours must do precisely what mine does. That's it. Bloody good. Jolly well. Clean the teeth and gums. Fine tongue on you. Halfway down my throat. Jesus. Careful. Make me throw up.

"Stop. Fielding, that's enough. Stop it. I see what you

mean. Let's finish our ribs." A bit of labored breathing.

"Swell idea, Lil."

"Sorry."

"Forget it. You're right. Pass the bag."

And flick on the tube to fill this room with something other than lust. Bozo the Clown for a start, patting the bottoms of almost winners, and Lil enjoying the antics. Me in a plastic chair in this tiny room, eating ribs in tomato paste, wondering where I am and who this is, wishing for a weak instant to be back among compatriots in familiar streets. The kidneys are better, now I'm off the hoof. Looks like Harris Paris in that Bozo suit. My poor friends, so eloquent in defeat. I must remember their trick in times of stress; Judgment Day, for instance. Need a touch to wash this taste away.

A quick greasy buss to Lily's cheek and Jones was down the rear stairs with dark glasses and trombone case to fool the law and keep the Brownies off. Across the avenue he slunk, into Goldfinger's liquor store where Isaac Goldfinger brought dusty bottles tumbling from a high shelf and charged a nickel for a bag to hide them in. Back to the door to face, through glass and chain link fence, a nasty child beckoning with forefinger. And nowhere to go but out.

"Excuse me, young lady. I'm late for a big recording session. No time for autographs."

"I recognize you, mister."

"You do?"

"Yup."

"Who am I?"

"That pervert we saw in the woods."

"I'd like to explain."

"The cops are after you."

"How was I to know Brownies were roaming the woods?"

96

"Not Brownies. Girl Guides."

"What's the difference?"

"We're underprivileged."

"Listen. I was sick. I had to do that."

"Don't worry. I got eight brothers." She tugged the tails of a dirty blouse. Little buds of breasts appearing.

"So you've seen such sights before."

"Yeah. That's about the biggest one I ever saw, though."

God, spare me from such children. A connoisseur at twelve.

"What's your name?"

"Winifred."

"Okay, Winifred. Are you going for a cop?"

"Naw."

"You aren't?"

"I don't think so."

"I appreciate that."

"Old camel breath just hates men. She pounded on that cop until he said he'd look for you."

"One cop?"

"Yeah."

"Well, thanks Winifred."

"Hey wait, mister."

"What."

"I keep my mouth shut for ten bucks."

"Ten bucks."

"And I'll tell them I saw you hop a bus for Kansas City."

"That's very un-Brownie-like."

"I'm underprivileged."

"Okay, Winifred. Five bucks. No more."

"Seven-fifty, you cheapskate."

"Five, you nasty little—"

"I'll scream, mister."

"Right. Here. Get lost."

"What's in the bag?"

"I'll scream, Winifred."

"See ya around, mister. Wish I was a few years older. Wow."

She stuffed the bills in a filthy saddle shoe and disappeared down the street into a cigar store. To buy dirty books and Lucky Strikes, no doubt, and corrupt that native innocence.

Jones trudged back, brain full of bogs and fens, spiders and fish guts. A cell might be the best place for me. It's safer than freedom and far more restful. Lily's up waiting in the room with that big anxious body, and I with a will of balsa. Better to hop a train now and leave all messes behind. Except for an errant duffel my miserable life depends on. Face the music and dance, Jones. Good things may be forthcoming, since you've near exhausted the bad.

He found Lily fast asleep, hands behind her head, breasts thrust up, legs slightly parted. Breathing gently. And one need only move this chair slightly to the left, about here, to glimpse up shanks and who knows what. Gently sleeping Lily, I'd be your blanket if you asked. Keep you cozily bundled. Lord, stop these eyes and thoughts. Long, muscular, milky thighs. Strange how dirty book descriptions seem to fit. Succulent ice cream scoops tipped with strawberries. Oh, Jesus. Hot, ripe, quivering melons. Giving me delirium tremens. Waving in an electric arc of passion, biting off earlobes, ripping strips of skin from backs. Room full of musk and perspiration. Quick pour a shot and watch the dregs of Bozo or I'll faint from lust.

He piled sofa cushions on the floor beneath Bozo's gamboling figure, set out DO NOT DISTURB signs, removed trousers with back to Lily. And tried his humble pallet, an extra blanket preserving modesty.

98

About the room the remains of ribs looked as though lions had been through. She was no cleaning fanatic, this one. Tip the glass and another Canadian courses down these guts, so often visited. How many bottles could one kill in a lifetime? Millions, in my case. For hooch doth elevate the soul.

> *And malt does more than Milton can*
> *To justify God's ways to man.*

Dark came slowly through the windows as Jones was wakened by gentle laughter.

"You're an indecent man."

"What?"

"At least your shorts are."

"I've come uncovered."

"They say 100% PURE LEAD on the seat."

"That's right. What of it?"

"It's funny."

"Well. I've run out of things to wear. No wife, you know."

"I'll wash them out in the sink."

"That won't be necessary."

"You sound tired. Look, it's after eleven."

"I need a bolus. My back aches and I'm three behind already. Wonder how those cops are doing."

Lily sat up in bed; his eyes twitched awake. About her broad, freckled shoulders and chest draped little laces of negligee. And a tiny silver chain hanging down between the mounds: a Catholic contraceptive peddler? Unlikely.

"You're in your nightie."

"I woke a few minutes ago and put it on. Some company I've been."

"It's very becoming."

"I'd show it to you, but I'm afraid it's transparent. Except here at the bodice."

"Won't think about that."

"I took advantage of your sleeping to get it on. In the morning I'll have to trust you to close your eyes."

"You will?"

"Fielding. Your left eye is twitching."

"I sleep with it open."

"I watched you while I was changing. It wasn't open."

So I've missed the main feature for need of a snooze. Curse this infirm body.

"Could I pour you anything?"

"What have you?"

"Dry Manhattan."

"I'm not sure."

"Mind me cavorting in my underwear?"

"I'm not sure."

"Close your eyes."

Up to the bathroom for two water glasses, Lily shocked, then giggling. Mix them fast with a lemon rind twisted, wondering if it wouldn't be to advantage to sleep in the skin instead of these sexless shorts, bought by Sarah in a rare risqué moment. No. Mustn't frighten her off when I've promised to be pure.

"Cheers, Lily."

"Excuse me, Fielding. I can't help it. You're hilarious."

"Oh."

"I didn't know men still wore sleeveless undershirts."

"Older men do." Some pain in the voice.

"I didn't mean that."

"It's all right."

"I've hurt your feelings. I'm so sorry."

"Never mind, Lily. Truth is truth."

100

"But your age means nothing to me. True age is measured in the heart. Not the body."

"At times the body."

"Not for me."

A little sorry to hear that news.

"You're a young man to me, Fielding."

"You're a gentle, sweet woman. Drink to our mutual admiration. And youthful hearts."

And as you lift your glass, I see tight dark circles glowing beneath that bodice you believe to be opaque. Little raspberries poking out the lace. Risen from the April chill. Or Jones romping about in underwear; vain thought.

"I'll return to my bower and cover up now. Cease this ridiculous display."

"Are you comfortable on the cushions?"

"A few cracks about the back is all."

"And you with a backache."

"Nothing new. I'd have one lying on heavenly clouds."

"You'll take the bed. I can sleep anywhere. I've slept in tents with South American Indians. I'm big and rugged."

"I'm big and rugged, too."

"I'm young and big and rugged."

"You have a point."

"Close your eyes and I'll change beds with you."

"No."

"Fielding?"

"No. I refuse. And if you mention my age again, I'll do something irrational."

"You're awfully touchy sometimes. And very stubborn."

"Or something dirty."

"No you won't. You promised."

"I can see through that nightgown, you know."

There's a flurry in the covers as she rushes to bury the

101

treasures. Why'd you tell her, Jones? Never a good peeper, I guess. Always had to touch what I looked at. Held mama's with two little hands, like a bottle.

"Oh! I really don't know you, Fielding. One moment you're lovely and the next you're awful."

"That's me."

"I insist you take this bed. And stop talking nasty."

"I was being honest. I could see right through."

"I'm not listening. Take this bed. I insist."

"Stop insisting or I'll remove my shorts. And do a horn-pipe."

"I'm not listening."

Jones tossed off the cover and stood up, removing his undershirt, thrusting thumbs in the elastic of his Fruit of the Looms.

"What are you doing?"

"Stripping for action."

And before 100% PURE LEADs hit the floor, Lily is buried in blankets above the eyes. Strange how nakedness will have its way. On with dark glasses so as not to be thought indecent. Out with this fine trombone, instrument of the gods. And I, the elusive unicorn, awaiting virgin's hands upon my horn, which only the pure of heart may touch. Standing on this chair should heighten the effect. A nifty little Highland fling, shuffle ball change, and a one two three, one two, one two three kick. Used to lindy up a storm in those palmy prewar days. They played real music then. No electric guitar and tambourine crap. Good sensible stuff which I'll demonstrate for her.

"Fielding! What is that noise?"

"I'm playing the trombone. Recognize it?"

"Are you dressed?"

"This may date me a bit."

"Fielding. Answer me."

" 'Flat Foot Floogie With the Floy Doy.' Quiet and listen to the chorus."

"Someone's pounding on the wall."

"Termites."

"Oh, God."

"Very possible."

"I don't believe it."

"Would you care for something more mellow? A bit of 'Cement Mixer, Puttee Puttee' ?"

"Go away. Just go away. You're terrible. I didn't do anything to you. I was nice to you. I trusted you, Fielding."

Mournful, muffled tones rose from under heaps of bedding. Play another or retreat to bed, Jones? It isn't working as before. Hell, one more for good measure. For the bastard beating on the wall, who apparently doesn't relish midnight solos. Now some noise from up above. Must have recognized the tune. Very nice percussion. In stereo, too.

"Stop or you'll have the police in here. Please, Fielding. For both our sakes."

"My repertoire is not yet exhausted."

"Stop this minute. I insist."

"There you go insisting. I'll play 'The Sheik of Araby.' Sing right along, Lil. Follow the bouncing balls."

Rising from the bed a smothered figure, mummified in sheets and blankets but for one large eye. It's the Phantom of the Opera, though with bumps no phantom ever owned. It stumbles off the bed, moving toward the stage whereon cavorts a glorious star, pumping his old trombone in merry abandon. That eye is looking where it shouldn't. And is suddenly very much wider than it was. Oh, oh. That's not nice. Wrenching a man's trombone from his lips. And taking it back to bed, buried where I would like to be.

"That wasn't kind, Lily."

"Get dressed, Fielding."

"You peeked."

"I didn't."

"My heart skips when I hear a lie."

"You'll have to be quiet now."

"I'm coming to get my trombone."

"You'd better not."

"Here I come, Lil."

"I'll do something. I'll scream."

"You've taken my instrument."

"Don't come any closer! Stop! I'll give it to you if you'll put something on."

"That's better. See how reasonably we can get along when we want to?"

"Will you please dress?"

"Certainly. I'm becoming decent at this very moment."

"Tell me when I can look."

"One moment. There. There. Let's check in the mirror now. Okay. Time. Come out, Lily. I'm ready."

"Oh!"

"Mustn't scream. Wake the neighbors."

"But you said you'd dress."

"I have on socks."

Small tears collect in the corners of eyes which seem reluctant to take shelter again. Jones shivers, suddenly very nude. Blankets peel down, hit the mattress in a heap, and strange things vibrate in the air.

"Oh, Fielding."

"I beg your pardon, Lily?"

"So many years and all at once it's here."

"Mustn't cry, Lily."

"My head feels hot. I can't help it. Come closer to me. I want to see you. Here, you can look at me."

Up over the head goes the snowy negligee, wherein lies

Miss Robertson's deepest secrets. And, all aghast, I sit down on the bed beside her. Tears splashing my knuckles. How much of you, Lily, the wool has hidden. Breasts I'd care to die between. My casket pillows. And mare's thighs, tight, large, muscled, parted for my eyes and never for another's. Yes, you may touch it, Lil. Cry on it, if you wish. It's yours now and this is mine. All these fleshy treasures. And I'll weep, too. On the inside. Warm these shivering bosoms on my tongue. As Sarah enjoyed me doing winter nights in Michigan because I wouldn't pay to heat the room. And though I am old and loose about the guts you've chosen me, me of all who have passed you days and nights, summer afternoons with lemonade fresh on your lips, and burned for what you've given just to one elderly fellow. I'd make me twenty-five for you, if I could, Lily. Then you'd have all the lust and love you deserved. Cry for the years, the hours, times sleeping, bored, and angry. Roll them up and give them back. Counting seconds till the blood's juices unbubble and go flat.

At the screens millers strum, tick like pebbles on the glass. David watched moths, I remember. Tiny, plump, half-buried eyes sifting light, sorting wings, seeking frail green silk of the luna, elusive as wind, silent goddess of all moths, moon moth. Moth of the moon. His tongue hung ecstatic when he saw it, the thick, dumb expression of his joy. And I wept at his little human moment as the wings sighed, sliding down winds, and beside the porch hydrangeas nodded ghostly heads. I held him. And he filled his pants. Lily. A piece of me gone now. Lie back and I'll teach you. It's my finest lecture. I'll expect notes. Much testing to assure me you've learned your lessons well.

"Oh, Lord."

"It's only me, Lily."

"Oh, Lord."

"Lily?"

"Oh, Fielding."

"Have you a sample from your basket?"

"Don't stop. Don't worry, darling."

"I believe I've won a point."

And in an instant I'm locked tight, enmeshed in muscles, hips, thighs, feet, bones, toes. Long, taut moments. Moans from an ordinarily proper maiden. And a scream. A little spot from your heart on the sheet. Deflowered forever by F. Jones, Esquire. Your largeness like a featherbed I'll lie in till I croak. Kneel beside to say my prayers. Dreams and fulfillments simultaneous.

"Oh, it's lovely."

"Is it?"

"Delicious."

"Oh."

"I want some chicken after. I'm ravenous."

"Leave it to the colonel."

And up into the air on a bucking pubis. How well you do what you haven't done before. No worries passing this course. Slower, though. Remember age and infirmities. Wonder if Sarah is watching from heavenly portholes. Weaving rugs with a fury, shaking fists. Funny to think. I'll hold these smooth haunches, Sarah, preferring them to where you are. My beautiful Lily Robertson, hungry beneath me. Empty tummy I'll help to fill. With babies, I fear. I could learn to love you, if I thought about it. Trapped here in your arms and legs. You close your eyes but I never do. Too much around to see. Your tongue stretching into canals of my ears. Make a living killing ants, if you wanted. Fingers squeezing one worn buttock. Feels so good. You make me feel a stallion, Lily, and under me my mare. I'm all young again, adrift in a fountain of youth. And out of you come noises that are horsy, strange. One

106

more look the length of you. Your little chain has a note on it, I see, resting just above one pinkish jelly bump. Says in red: I AM AN EPILEPTIC.

"My God."

Much writhing and unusual utterings from below. Old de Sade might enjoy this but not a Christian gentleman.

"Lily."

"Oh-h-h."

"Lily!"

"It's happening. Move, Fielding."

"What's happening? Should I put a towel in your mouth?"

"Oh, darling."

"You're all right?"

"Yes, yes."

"God. You gave me a flutter."

"Oh!"

And together we deliver our urgent exhortations, proving for science and the world that one organ will endure when the heart itself has failed. So, Lily, like the rest of us you are marked. Your long-preserved virginity I begin to understand. Worms won't try it first, dear Lil. I've beat the bastards to it.

"Fielding."

"What, Lil."

"Hold me close tonight."

"I will, Lily."

Then in my ear she begins to weep. Weeps I love you, Fielding, with breath so soft it's ticklish.

And long, long after little wet lines dry on my chest and eyes and tears cease in sleep, I watch the words, tiny elfin children in fields of weeds. Capering on my brains.

14

Day came at half past six with Lily's breath on his neck, and her tongue moving in the crevasses and over the bristles twenty-four hours had brought. Her big thigh lay heavy across him. Outside, the hissing of street sweepers mopping up, shouts of a newsman echoing on bricks and stones. Cry of a horn and smell of peanuts roasting in Goldfinger's window. And from the interior man a fear leaped up; hypochondriacal fogs swept the brain. Fear of death by flesh. Charge the duffel thief with murder, too.

"Hello, Fielding."

"Uh."

"You're very clammy. Are you feeling all right?"

"Uh uh."

"Fielding. You're sick. Lie still. I have a thermometer in my case."

And out she bounded, naked and flexing. Through burn-

109

ing eyes Jones watched her bend to rifle through underwear and papers and toss them about the floor. Sweet
round bottom it was, pink from rubbing sheets. Red
strands of hair brushed her shoulders, and breasts, pendu-
lous, pointed down. I'd like to be a Mounty now. Sergeant
Preston of the Yukon. God grant an ounce of strength.
Mush.

"Oral or rectal, Fielding?"

"Moo."

"You're up."

"Snort."

"Hey, stop that. Keep this under your tongue for two
minutes."

"I'll chew it up."

"Better wait then."

"Snort."

"Oh, Toro."

"Oink."

"Oh, Fielding."

"Oh-h-h. Good grief . . ." The floor suddenly rose to
meet his skull. El Toro lay felled and oozing. Carpet peo-
nies pressed his ear; plaster cracks blurred, multiplied at
a disturbing rate. Staring through rheumy eyes, he saw
webs covering walls and ceiling. Nausea swept through as
the nostrils found a little pile of rotting spareribs under
a chair. And everything went floating, slanted; unfocusing
in a ghastly ballet. Jones stumbled in the revolving barrel
of the fun house, his long naked body flopping about the
staves. Lily watched frightened above, pale and bare, still
prickling with desires. Damned in the midst of paradise.
Time is up, Jones. Up the account. Humping in the final
hour. Right to the death. There's a picture for the saints.
Instead of earnest supplication for previous errors, a
hearty, bullish snort from rear mount position number 32.

110

It's fear and trembling now. Get down and pray, Lil, while I try for the toilet on all fours.

"Fielding. What is it?"

"Go. Bathroom."

"Can't you walk? Tell me. I'll go for a doctor. You must get into bed. I'll help you up."

"Go. Bathroom. Puke."

"Why can't you walk?"

"Floor moves. Crawl. Puke."

"Poor Fielding. I'll get the door."

"Thank you."

"Certainly."

"Snort."

The can daily became a more faithful companion. He stared in its large eye, holding tight. The only point of stability in a disjointed world. My God, I'm dying sure as shit. Pray to Jesus, Mary. Any one of you guys listening. Sorry for all the things I've pulled. Couldn't help so much of it. My soul cast out red and chunky on the waters. Swirling out the hole and down six flights to God knows where. Ah, Sarah, give me a hand now. Out on the streets sirens blare and Lily shuts the door to leave me alone in my grief. Whom will I ever see again? Faces passing in the water's mirror. Father, I'd hoped we'd meet to fish in heavenly streams, but I see everlasting droughts for any lines of mine. Lord, what have I caught? Never had such disoriented feelings before. Room won't stay still, and now Lily's out there screaming. Loud shouting voices, too. Hang on to my toilet for dear life. Chaos cometh.

"Where is he? We know he's in here."

Lily sobbing: "You . . . you beasts! You villains! Get out of here! You can't just break in. I'll take you to court. My father has lawyers. You'll regret this. Stop leering at me. Give me my robe."

111

"Hey, Lieutenant. I never saw anything like that before. Even in Calumet City."

"Give her the robe, Sack."

"Yes sir. Too bad. Here lady."

"Get your filthy eyes off me!"

"We know he's in here, Miss Robertson. He gave us your name."

"What are you talking about. You're all insane! You'll pay for this! You can't just bust into somebody's room any time you please. I'll have your jobs for this! You bastards!"

"Easy, lady. Where's your friend."

"What friend?"

"Jones. Or whatever his name really is."

"Mr. Jones? What do you want with him? He's sick."

"Freaked out, Lieutenant."

"Shut up, Sack."

"Sir?"

"He's in here, isn't he."

"What if he is. He's sick. I've been taking care of him."

"Sure, lady."

"Shut up, Sack."

"Christ, sir."

"Where is he, Miss Robertson?"

"In the bathroom. Where else could he be. He's throwing up."

"Bad trip. I told you, Lieutenant."

"Sack . . ."

Jones stared at his reflection in the toilet, at the old sad eyes and dripping nostrils. The sagging lower lip. In the midst of silent prayer, he distantly recognized the clatter of a door flung wide and the movement of several feet nearby. He glanced down at the hard, black eyes of a military shoe and unavoidably threw up on it.

"Hey! The bastard! My new brogues!"

112

"Use the towel, Sack."

"Keep your hands off that towel. This is my room. Fielding, tell him to use his own towel."

"Uh."

"Use toilet paper, Sack."

"I should use the bastard's shirt."

"You use his shirt and I'll call the governor. Let me get a blanket for you, Fielding. Look at him shake. Can't you see he's burning up with fever?"

"Does he usually get sick in the raw, lady?"

"Lieutenant, I find the mouth of this young man offensive and impertinent."

"Shut up, Sack. Take the toilet paper and wait in the other room."

"What if they try to jump you, sir?"

"Then I'll scream, Sack, and you come running in."

"Right, Lieutenant. I'll be ready."

"Don't scream. He might kill us all."

"You watch it, lady. You're in this as deep as he is."

"Go, Sack. Close the door behind you."

Jones heard the latch but couldn't raise his head to look. This girl has rare reserves of spunk one would never recognize from looking.

"All right, Jones. Finish puking and get dressed."

"He needs a doctor, Lieutenant. You should be able to perceive that."

"He'll have one, Miss Robertson. As soon as we're done booking him."

"Booking him? On what charge? I suppose you took the word of that frustrated Brownie."

"Brownie? Was that him too? Whatta you know."

"Uh."

"Oh, heavens, Fielding. I'm sorry."

"Could I ask you something, lady?"

113

"What have I done, Fielding?"

"Why are you two in the buff?"

"We spent the night together. That's our business. We're two single, consenting adults."

"How long have you known Mr. Jones?"

"One day."

God forgive me, Lily. Keep the chin high and trembling from the voice. Your dignity plucks the heartstrings.

"What's your business at this hotel?"

"I'm a group leader in the national birth control convention."

"That's interesting."

"Your irony is not necessary, Lieutenant. By the way, do you have a warrant for Mr. Jones's arrest? If you don't, you can be on your way."

"Right here, Miss Robertson."

"What's the charge?"

"Possession of narcotics. We'll forget the indecent exposure for now."

"What?"

Lily. The starch suddenly gone from your voice and my heart.

"We found his duffel behind a couch in the lobby. With a package of heroin in it."

"Oh my God. Fielding. This isn't true."

"Uh."

"Tell me, Fielding."

"Uh."

"You'll have to come along for a few questions, Miss Robertson."

"Lieutenant! Stop him! He's trying to drown himself!"

"For God's sake, Jones. Out of that toilet right now. Put the seat down, Miss Robertson. You help him get dressed. I'll wait in the other room."

114

Lily, I'm sick. Heroin in my bag. Indecent exposure. Too sick to talk. Must be insanity setting in. I wasn't trying to kill myself. Thought it might revive me. I'll drown in a sea of tomatoes before I get to jail. Can't speak, Lil. Have to hang on to something. The world is off its axis. Feel like a dervish stuck in gear. Hold your big legs for safety in the storm. As you tearfully stuff me into underwear and make me decent. Decent for burial. Who unleashed the furies all at once? When only hours before I labored in the vineyards between these heavenly gateposts. Will I never lie there again? Weep. Weep. Your chimneys I sweep, and in soot I sleep.

> *Then naked and white, all my bags left behind,*
> *I rise upon clouds and sport in the wind;*
> *And the Angel told me, if I'd be a good boy,*
> *I'd have God for my father, and never want joy.*

I see bass leaping in the stream, Lily, and all the golden pools of sun. Children whole and clean upon the shore with crayfish in their jars. Like Charles Lamb's children. And a woman with moons for eyes. And silk for hair. And I, stout fellow, adrift beneath an ancient tree, lulled by sweet, human ambience. Amen.

15

Jones grunted and opened his eyes. From across the room, Jesus looked, slipping his heart out for Jones to see. It bled in bright puce.

"Fielding. I've come for you."

"Uh."

"I've come to take you home."

"Forgive me, for I have sinned."

"I shan't judge."

"You shan't?"

"No."

"I always figured you would."

"I may have difficulty explaining things."

"I understand."

"To the trustees."

"Are there trustees?"

"Of course. Who else?"

"Just like on earth."

117

"What?"

"Just like on earth."

"I thought you said that. I'm afraid I miss your irony."

"What irony?"

"Trust me. I'll help you."

"My light. Yes. I'll follow, Lord."

"Fielding?"

"Our Father who art in . . ."

"Fielding, for heaven's sake. What's gotten into you. It's me. Me."

Blinking through film distorting God's gushing heart, Jones saw.

"Dean Vredevelt? Dean. Good God. Where am I?"

"Here. In Des Moines."

"I'm still in Des Moines?"

"Yes, Fielding. You've been very ill. You're in St. Mary's Hospital. When I got the lieutenant's message, I flew here immediately."

"Still in Des Moines."

"You've been cleared of the heroin business. I thank God for that. You're not free to go just yet. There seems to be another charge."

"Indecent exposure."

"Yes." The Dean clutched his wool muffler in a sweaty hand. "For heaven's sake, Fielding, how do you do it? How do you manage such embroilments in so short a time?"

Sense a well-hidden, festering irritation there. How the skull doth throb.

"Sorry, Dean. I seem to have become your personal cross."

"Not all that bad, Fielding. If we can't clear this up, though, we'll both be in trouble."

"Could be my job."

"Very possibly."

118

"Good grief, Dean, would you mind turning that picture to the wall. It disturbs me."

"It is rather garish."

"Makes me feel all upchucky again. That bleeding heart assaults the dendrites."

Outside, a muscular nurse passed with a steaming bed-pan, stopped, peered in, mumbled something to an officer whose right arm was visible at the door.

"What happened to me?"

"You've had what the doctor calls vertigo. It's an inner ear infection which upsets the sense of balance. A kidney infection, too. I understand you've been delirious for twenty-four hours."

"This is a private room, Dean. My insurance only covers ward."

"For heaven's sake, Fielding. Stop worrying about inessentials. There's an officer at the door, you know."

"I see."

"Yes."

"Woe is me."

Jones propped his pillow and sat up. Looked through the window at a bleak, midmorning sky. A few pigeons clucked outside on the sill. Their plump breasts reminding him of Lily.

"Has there been a young lady in to see me, Dean?"

"Not that I'm aware of."

"A large, marish type; very virtuous looking."

"No, Fielding."

"Shit."

"What?"

"Shit."

In at the door came a familiar voice. A gaunt face of old zit marks, looking as if chickens had been feeding on it. Wheels clattered down a hall and someone wept beneath

119

a sheet. Inside the brain, bones rattled unpleasant melodies. This is Lazarus, come from the dead, they sang. Come back to tell you all . . .

"Well, Mr. Jones, you're awake."

"I'm not sure. You're the officer who prevented my drowning."

"You remember."

"Couldn't forget such gallantry."

The Lieutenant moved to the foot of the bed, resting a folded paper on his chin. "You've been cleared of the narcotics charge, Mr. Jones. We got word this morning that some small-time pusher slipped the stuff to you on a train to Chicago."

"A faith healer?"

"That's the guy."

My old friends. Selling me down the river though I'd unselfishly shared my spirits and played them tunes.

"There's this other matter, though, Mr. Jones." He opened the paper and took out bifocals from a vest pocket.

"I'm aware of it. I plead innocent."

"You seem to be caught regularly with your pants down."

"Just lately."

"What happened in the park?"

"They came upon me in an unfortunate moment. I was relieving myself."

"Miss Wolpot claims you made no attempt to cover yourself."

"Who's she?"

"The Girl Guide troop leader."

"It is difficult to dress with a mad woman attacking."

"She's a terror, I'll admit."

"Poor Fielding. Why don't you learn to avoid such indiscretions?"

120

"It's the kidneys, Dean."

"Lieutenant, believe Mr. Jones. He has a chronic kidney malfunction. Similar problems have occurred in the past."

Careful old man. That's dangerous ground.

"Would you mind explaining that, Mr. Vredevelt?"

The Dean folded his hands behind his back, turning with sad eyes toward Jesus' backside. "It occurred once under the bleachers at a football game. And once out fishing on the ice."

"What's that, Dean?"

"Fielding, I've never told you this. You've never made department chairman, you know. Even though I consider you better qualified than our present chairman . . ."

"Go on."

"You see, the night of October 14, 1959, at our annual homecoming game, one of the trustees' wives sitting in the bleachers, happened to be reaching down for a fallen purse when she—"

"Tell me no more."

"—caught a glimpse. On another occasion at Pickerel Lake—"

"Oh, come on. Everybody pisses on the ice, Dean."

"But not everybody is seen by Mrs. DeJong."

"I hope it was exhilarating."

"Please, Fielding."

"Well, now I know. Why didn't you tell me before?"

"I couldn't bring myself to."

"You're a kind man. Can't say much for the rest of the Pharisees. Bastards."

The Lieutenant cleared his throat and set his glasses down the nose. "Well, Mr. Jones. There's a way out. This is a statement Miss Wolpot has asked me to read."

121

"Forged in blood."

"No. Very masculine hand, though. Let me read:

Mr. Fielding Jones
Suspected Exhibitionist

Mr. Jones:

All charges against you will be dropped if you will formally apologize for your actions before the Des Moines Exalted Council of the Girl Guides of America, on Wednesday, April 30, at 8 P.M. at the Rudolph Hotel. If you choose not to, you can expect to be hounded and harassed until justice is meted out to my satisfaction—which means to the full letter of the law and more.

R.S.V.P.

> *Yours Truly,*
> *Grinelda W. Wolpot*
> *Troop Leader*
> *Pack 69*
> *Girl Guides of America*
> *Des Moines, Iowa*

Oh essence of Christian femininity. Gloating at misfortune. Contented only when she has me mewling and puking at those steel reinforced feet. Expediency demands it, I can sense. Even the constable sympathizes. But his eyes say there's no choice. Life is full of such reductions of being. What's one more to one so beaten upon.

"Take a letter, Lieutenant."

"Shoot, Mr. Jones."

Miss Grinelda W. Fullpot
Suspected Voyeur

Dear Miss Fullpot:

The Exalted Council sounds delightful. I shall address it with appropriate vigor. I only hope I can maintain the kind of interest I did at our first encounter. I shall not forget the look in your eyes.

> *Affectionately,*
> *F. Jones, Esquire*

"Perhaps the lieutenant could edit that a bit, Fielding."

"Deliver it verbatim, if you please, Lieutenant."

"It's your neck, Mr. Jones. Spell *voyeur.*"

"It's not wise, Fielding."

"Then it is quite in accord with the majority of my actions, Dean. V-O-Y-E-U-R. Tugboat Annie wants to make all the rules. No thanks. I'll take my chances. Officer O'Malley, what's become of Miss Robertson?"

"Sullivan is the name. Spell council."

"C-O-U-N-C-7-I-L. What's become of Miss Robertson?"

"C-O-U-N-C what?"

"IL, Lieutenant. Just IL. Miss Robertson. Where is she?"

The Lieutenant pummeled a word with his eraser and blew dirty little rubber rolls across the bedsheets. "Never knew how to spell. Have to be careful with an English teacher around."

"Right, Lieutenant. Now—"

"She had a fit in the patrol car."

"What? Epilepsy?"

"Tore up the cruiser. Nearly put a foot right through the

123

back window. When she didn't come out after fifteen minutes, we ran her up to emergency."

"Where is she?"

"Checked out of St. Mary's this morning. We didn't hold her."

"Did she leave a message?"

"No."

"She doesn't know I'm cleared."

"Probably not."

"Life is beautiful."

"What is it, Fielding?"

"Nothing, Dean. Nothing."

Our nada who art in nada, hallowed be thy nada. One happy ending and I'd give my heart to You. Happiness, illusion of illusions, conjured up by monoliths like me. Candides. Feigning joy while the grief heaps up. Pigeons at my windows I wish were breasts to place my head upon. Gaunt spring trees are Novemberish, grim. Your gentle heart, Dean, won't pump out this sinking ship. Not this time.

"I can't go back with you, Dean. If they give you trouble, I'll resign. Maybe. Hate to lose that sabbatical money." Crawling from bed, Jones trembled and held a steel table. A thermometer crashed on the gray tiles.

"Reconsider, Fielding. You have great ability in difficult situations. Your chances are much better in person."

"Can't, Dean. I have things to do. I've got to see my son."

"What are you doing?"

"Looking for clothes."

"I don't believe you've been released yet. Has he, Lieutenant?"

"Where are my things?"

"In the closet, Mr. Jones. You'll have to get an official release form."

124

"I'll get it."

Fumbling into wrinkled trousers and starchless shirt, a hospital robe for underwear, Jones choked back nausea and outrage. Beneath his shoes the duffel of medicines, like an old friend, offered up its handles.

"Fielding, you aren't well enough."

"This bag is all I need."

He lurched out the room and down the corridor, the robe hanging untucked behind and through unbuttoned spots. Nurses stared. "Sir? Aren't you a patient of ours?"

"Fire inspector. I've found a hazard I must report." He noticed as he reached the stairway that he'd forgotten socks.

"Wait a minute. Aren't you Mr. Jones with the vertigo?"

"Name is Smith with Fireman's Mutual."

Into the solitude of a fire route. No one uses stairs in a hospital. A man could be mugged and not found for weeks. Still the fourth floor. A thousand steps to go and strength is ebbing. The twelve labors of Hercules were nothing like this. Maybe I can lie on the banister and ease myself down . . .

Shooting toward the landing, Jones screamed and became a sudden gutsy heap. He rolled to a corner and groaned; pills, bottles, underwear lay in profusion on the steps. His heart beat desperately, rushing life to the extremities. Getting to his knees, he moved to gather up the losses.

"Fielding! Are you down there?"

"No, Dean."

"The nurses say you aren't well enough to leave. They've gone down to the first floor to catch you."

"I've never felt better. Good-bye, Dean."

"Fielding. Wait."

Out on floor two and down through aisles of squalling infants. A mother in a breast pump gave a little snort and

125

Jones quickened his pace. At the nurses he nodded professionally.

"Hey. What are you doing? Visiting hours aren't till one."

"Pardon me. I'm wanted in surgery."

A fat one doesn't believe it. Shouldn't have forgotten the socks. Sense footsteps close behind, gaining. A city of red and black babies. Never saw so many. I looked at David through windows like these and saw his strange little limbs. Sarah never wept but I did at home, into many beers. Afterward we bought Charles, for safety's sake. If I died would Charles come to see?

"You! Stop this instant!"

Through signless doors he flew. And before him the shiny wet head of a baby coming out. A doctor looked up with angry eyes.

"Who the hell are you? Get out!"

"Excuse me, Dr. Fielding Jones at your service. Is this the Schultz appendectomy?"

"Hell no. Does it look like it?"

"Pardon me. Must have taken a wrong turn. Which way is out?"

"The way you came in."

"Is there an alternate route?"

"Nurse, call an orderly."

"Yes, doctor."

"Those orange doors, for example."

"Out!"

No time for answers. Try the orange ones anyway. Into the antiseptic steel glint of the recovery room, nodding to pale smiling new mothers with plastic tubes in their arms.

"Feeling better, Mrs. Schultz?"

"Yes, thank you, doctor. I'm Mrs. Reed."

126

"Fine baby you have."

"I had an appendectomy."

"Quite right. Good day, Mrs. Schultz."

"Good day, doctor."

Allah be praised, not a nurse in sight. But in a room across the hall a body sheeted tip to toe. A sudden freeze, and zero in the bones. Sign says lobby this way, down one flight. With a little luck I'm out and free. Find Lily and she can make me well. I think that guy was dead, all right. Lord.

Jones peeked out the iron door into the lobby. An ancient guild lady was selling trinkets. OUTPATIENT EXIT shown in red over large glass doors manned by a pretty black nurse checking release forms.

He straightened his few hairs, tucked all loose edges under his belt, and calmly strode to the check-out desk. A dark, evil-looking little woman approached him.

"Could I help you?"

"Yes. I need a release form for a patient of mine."

A piercing eye searched him up and down. "Do I know you?"

"Perhaps not. I am Dr. Fielding Jones."

"I've never seen you before."

"I am a specialist from Michigan. I was called in last night on an emergency."

"What is your specialty?"

"Brains and dangling participles."

"I see. You'll have to wait a moment while I clear this with the business manager."

"Madam, I want that form this instant. If you refuse, I shall see the business manager myself about your inefficiency. I am in the midst of an emergency. There is no time to dally. A man may be dying because of you."

"But—"

127

"Where is the manager?"

"Wait. Here's the form. I'm only doing my job like I'm told to."

"You must learn to respond to emergency situations or you are of no value to a hospital staff. Sign that, please."

"Yes, doctor."

"And let's pray our patient hasn't—"

"Oh, don't say it! I'm signing."

And over to the men's room to forge the rest. Jones started at the ashen figure in the mirror. Picture of Dorian Gray. The days and nights have taken a toll. Bagged, bloodshot orbs. Seen corpses with aliver looks. Death's second self, Jones, the reflection of the real thing. Try a little water on the lids and storm the door. One pretty, smooth-thighed chocolate nurse to go.

"Good morning, my dear. I'm leaving today. My release." The sun flashed through a flying cloud and struck the glass.

Deep brown eyes turned up to him. "You can't be released without an escort."

"She was unfortunately detained on the elevator. A woman seemed to be having some kind of fit."

"Good heavens. Do they need help?"

"I believe they do. She was a very large woman."

"I'll only be a moment. Will you wait?"

"Certainly, my dear. You see to your duty."

And I'll see to mine.

Jones stumbled into the street, crossed through raging autos, slipped on a crosstown bus rocketing, he prayed, toward somewhere recognizable.

16

Three buses and two hours later, Jones found himself in a familiar lobby gripping his duffel tight to his side. Life's juices ebbing, he propped himself at the desk and hit the bell once weakly. The clerk inched warily forward from an interior office.

"Hello, sport. Did they let you out?"

"I've been cleared."

"Well, that's a relief. Drugs are bad publicity. Almost rather have a murder. Boy, you look like you just got out of Auschwitz. Were they rough on you?"

Jones let lids fall momentarily over his burning eyes.

"Is Miss Robertson still here?"

"No, sport. She checked out this morning. Whole day early. I don't blame her. The harpies were having a field day at her expense. Hey, that was dirty pool, staying overnight with her and not letting us know. I bumped her bill up six bucks on account of it. You shouldn't do that, sport.

Hey. Something else. She said she'd put your luggage in a locker at the train station."

"Did she leave a message?"

"Message? Yeah. Believe she did."

"Could I have it, please?"

"Lemme see. Here it is. No, you can't."

"Give me it, dammit. I'll crack your skull."

The clerk backed off in the direction of the telephone. "Hey, sport. Settle down. You try and sock me and you'll have a heart attack. You oughta see a doctor. No kidding."

"Give me the note."

"No."

"I'm losing patience. I'll tear out your nostrils."

"It isn't for you. I'd give it to you if it was."

"It isn't?"

"It's addressed to Mildred Hopp, Conference Chairman. That's the chief hag."

"Oh."

"Sorry, sport."

"I apologize."

"Forget it."

"You're a bastard for charging her six dollars extra. You know that."

"Well, gee. That's the policy around here."

"It stinks."

"All right, it stinks. So what."

"Bastard."

"You better get out or I'll call the bell captain."

"He's a bastard, too."

"Yeah, but he's a big bastard. Archie!"

The clerk hit the bell hard and retreated to the office. The bell captain lumbered up, arms bulging in a red jacket, grinning dully at Jones.

130

"Get your bag, sir?"

"That won't be necessary. I'm not staying. Tell the clerk for me that he's a bastard."

"Better watch your language in here, bud." He moved his little round cap back on his head. Muscles tortured his coat seams.

The clerk returned to the desk and began doodling with a ballpoint on the register. "Archie, this is the man who caused all the trouble the other night. Would you please escort him to the nearest exit."

"Sure, Mr. Avis."

"Touch me and you'll regret it. My hands are deadly weapons."

"Yeah, I can see that. So are wet noodles."

"Hands off me, you palooka. You damned jocks are all alike. Ouch. Unbend my arm or I'll scream."

"Go ahead."

"Aiee-e-e-e-e!"

"Hey, cut it out."

Heads leaned out of the restaurant and a maid dropped a load of towels. All eyes in the lobby faced front.

"Let me go or I'll do it again."

"Okay. But you get way out of here."

"I was thinking of having lunch."

"You—"

"—but I won't. I understand the food is better across the street. At the mission."

"Make tracks."

"I make footprints in the sands of time."

"Move."

"Ruffian. Whey face."

"Okay—"

"Touch and I'll shatter the chandeliers with my falsetto. You stand warned."

"Archie! Stop!"
"Aie-e-e-e-e!"

Jones opened his eyes to find his skull on the pavement, his face reflected in a Ford hubcap. His duffel lay beside him, reeking of rubbing alcohol. He placed the bag beneath his left ear. Broken glass clinked, as he undoubtedly would standing. Shattered pieces of old bones rattling within. Rib cage and ego crushed at once.

People looked from passing cars and shook their heads. Jones, slowly lifting himself, felt tears well in his eyes. His chest ached. His head reeled as he watched the face in the hubcap elongate and disappear. Across the street a sign blinked. GUIDING LIGHT MISSION—HOPE FOR THE HOPELESS, and the neon bad in all the Ps.

He crossed the street and rested against a mailbox. On all the street no bird sang. Strange. Where are the birds when you need them? Above bricks and windows blew heavy clouds, black Octoberish clouds, full of snows and omens. Lightning snapped at a radio tower and a large raindrop slapped Jones's ear; he moved beneath the Rudolph's long green awning.

Thinking, Charles. Son of mine. All that's left but mother. And mother unapproachable. Unless Jesus came into my heart and made me a lamb like DeJong. God. I'd let Him in if He'd leave me alone. To be me and no fossilized, grinning goodie. Lily, why did you leave? Big, firm, resolute girl. Things I saw in Sarah once. Strange, it's so easy to forget the early Sarah. Up to the hips in a stream with me, catching carp. Hating it. Loving me. Where was I? Where am I? Under an awning under a cloud, nauseated and quivering. Going fast. Finding nothing. Nothing everywhere I grab. Charles lives somewhere toward the west. Charles, who doesn't know me. Whom I love but do

132

not know. All the strength gone out of me. And no birds.

Rain pounded suddenly on canvas and pavement. Behind him the bell captain grimly watched. Down the Street YMCA shown scarlet through the dark. Hospital of the poor in spirit, club of the lonely hearts, where I should go to sleep back health and heart.

And with a large breath, he pushed himself out into the deluge and was instantly pummeled.

In the dismal yellow light of a tenth-story single, Jones watched humanity crawl. The coming and going of little men on paths of no note. Downward lies the way. My soul low and lower. Never lower. I always wondered why Christian men jumped from YMCA windows. Now I know. This thin steel bed with a little green lamp beside. Evidence on the nightstand that the Gideons had been here. There was faith in action. But Jones's charity was always Jones. A picture of Jesus in a field of children hung on the opposite wall. One child's head felt the caress of that gentle hand. Looks like little Charlie from a distance. And I, so unlike that other being. More of an Old Testament type, I guess. Old Job Jones. Moaning and covered with boils, all things taken away, consoled by no friends, not even false. Pick up this black book and peruse his story once more. The wizard of Uz. Innocently condemned to savor suffering, serene in despair, wanting only a hearing and an umpire. A judge to find out why.

> *As for man, the son of woman, his days are short and full of trouble.*
> *He comes out like a flower, and is cut down: he goes in flight like a shade, and is never seen again.*

God, what inspiration. Savor our blossoming while we may. And at our little time devour.

There are people, a few, whom I love with my heart and would not hurt. I have harmed no man that I can recall. Sarah, perhaps, but I paid. Flowers have been known to bloom before shadows creep. My little space, my little flowering, I've loved, I've prized and filled. With a few delicious things. And many troubles. So many troubles. Rationalize the errors, Jones. Remember boyhood dreams of Jesus coming in a cloud and taking everyone but you. Sweating in that dark bed till a car passed by in the midnight streets, assuring the existence of at least one other being on the earth. Won't forget that horror soon.

Jones closed the book and lay back on the squeaking bed. Rain sounded lightly on streets below, and tires skied on puddles. Jones shivered and removed his clothing, a soggy heap on the tiles. Sheets were damp and cold; he fished a blanket from beneath the bedside table and spread it over him.

Forever I'll see my joy destroyed. Hands full of ashes. Heart cold, empty as this room. Old. Trousers rolled. Grave's a fine and private place, but none I think do there embrace. Was a girl from Kansas City. Had a gundrop on her titty. She could sing. She could dance. She had a moustache . . . .

134

17

Jones awoke to a pale, thousand-year-old face and the overwhelming breath of half-digested Thunderbird. He looked into crinkled, merry eyes glistening with rheum.

"You dead?"

"Who are you?"

"Ezekiel."

"Not again. Another illusion."

"First time I've been in here."

"Come to warn me."

"That's right."

"What have I done?"

"You've been here three hours past check-out time."

Jones blinked and glanced about the room. "What time is it?"

"Two."

"What day is it?"

"Wednesday."

"Good Lord."

"You shouldn't swear in a Christian place."

"Excuse me. Will I be charged?"

"No, sir. You've been sick."

"I have."

"Some hair of the dog?"

"No thanks, friend."

"It generally fixes me."

"I'm sick in a different way."

"I understand. I've been janitor here for eighteen years. I can see you're a man with an aching heart."

"That's part of it."

"I'll bet you left your old lady."

"Mine died."

"That's too bad. I have communion wine hidden in the linens."

"You're a kind man, but no thanks."

"Your sheets are soaked. You've been quite sick."

"How do I get to the train depot?"

"Ten blocks down, three blocks right. Are you going out in such shape? Have any money?"

"Enough to do me."

"Aren't you going to eat?"

"I'm not hungry." Stomach small and tight. I couldn't remember the last meal.

"Hold on. I'll get you something. A man can't travel on an empty stomach. Especially a sick man."

And he was out the door before Jones could answer. He dragged himself from bed, feeling weak, old. Tongue was dry in the cheeks. Beard sprouting white and itching. The sky was slate, heavy, but rainless; one tree far down the street seemed inclined to awaken in spite of the earth. New blood surged in the winey branch tips; small knobs shown on limbs and fingers. Earth's bowels were healthier

136

than his, from which even a hair was hard put to gain sustenance. His shorts, lost down the leg of his trousers, were still damp; he dressed without them. The Pure Leads lay in a locker at the depot, folded and placed in a case by the hands of Lily Robertson. You shouldn't have gone, Lil. I wasn't what you thought. My oddities delighted you and age seemed no matter. When the shaft rose and did its work. Things in a case touched by you. Never wash them. Smell your fresh scent on my sundries. Remember you dressing me on the bathroom floor. Our last moment alone and you wept. For all you had given freely to an imposter, you thought. And now gone forever. The Super Chief speeding you toward somewhere near Chicago. And I never asked where. Pray for a gentle train wreck. A minor catastrophe . . .

Jones tore out his wallet and read the front of his ticket:

C&O Railroad passage round trip, Eel River to Denver, a maximum of four stops en route allowable. Any change of reservation must be made twenty-four hours in advance.

H. P. Sauce
Stationmaster

Twenty four hours in advance. Down the hall to the phone book to find the hotels, motels, and missions. There's a thousand if there's one. Try the classy joints. She'll be there if I know Lil. Patrician upbringing is never squeezed entirely out. Six dimes in my pocket. That's shocking good luck. Holiday Inn first, and then Howie J. Without results. Park Place sounds like class. Until the desk clerk spoke with the careful precision of an AA candidate. Two others

137

failed and only a dime remained. YWCA. There's a long shot. Slip it in the slot and dial. Listen. A knell. That summons me to heaven, or . . .

"Yes? Central YWCA."

"Madam. I'm calling for a young women I believe is staying there. Her name is Lily Robertson."

"One moment, sir."

An audible stir behind the scene; the voice returned.

"Excuse me, sir. May I ask who is calling, please?"

"The Duke of Des Moines."

"One moment please."

Jones shredded a cigarette filter and buried it in sand.

"Sir. Miss Robertson is standing here about to check out. She wants to know who this really is."

"Tell her it's Lieutenant Sullivan of the Des Moines police."

"Yes sir."

A moment's pause as the receiver bumped from hand to hand.

"Hello? Lieutenant?"

"Lily, you've got to listen to me—"

"Fielding?"

"Lily, I'm not what you think. Please—"

The receiver clicked down, the line dead.

"Ezekiel!"

From a room down the hall a worried voice. "Is that you, Mr. Jones? What's the matter? Say, Mr. Jones. I have ham and eggs frying. Come here a minute. I'd like you to see my place."

Jones flew to him and in through the door. Momentarily stunned, he glanced about at a thousand little plaster saints and angels ornamenting the sills, tables, floor. Ham on the air was sweet; his stomach winced at the lack of it. Pictures of prophets covered the walls and two huge orange eyes peered down from the ceiling.

138

"God, Ezekiel. Your place is overrun with holiness."

"Be cautious, Mr. Jones. This is God's house as much as any church. Don't profane it."

"I beg your pardon. Those two eyes. They look like somebody's tiger burning bright."

"Not a tiger, Mr. Jones. God's eyes."

"Right over your bed?"

"He's always looking."

"Quite right, Ezekiel. Tell me something. I'm in a hurry. Where is Sterling Street?"

"Down front."

"This is Sterling?"

"I ought to know."

"Where is the YWCA?"

"Right there," pointing out the window.

"I never saw it."

"Your window doesn't face Sterling."

"I'll be back. Keep the ham warm and sign me for another night. You're a fine man, Ezekiel. Saintlier than all of these."

"You aren't going now."

"Got to. But I'll return to keep you company. Your thoughts are Christian, sir."

And down long, unfamiliar beige hallways of dark little doors. He found an elevator which took only a moment to reach him. Luck was surging backward in his direction. The operator was a young black with a shaved head and psoriasis crusting on the scalp.

"Lobby, please. Full speed."

"Can't go no faster than this thing will take us."

"Do your best."

"I always do my best, boss."

"Boy, that's an ugly scalp you've got. I have some stuff up in my room I'll lend you. Called Selsun. Fix you up in three days."

"Man, don't you go signifying on my scalp. I'll leave your ass in the basement."

Jones thumped a foot in time to the elevator chains. "You like that grot on your head?"

"Yeah, I like it."

"Suit yourself."

"Thanks, man. Nice leaving you."

The doors opened onto the lobby. Old men, semiderelicts, lounged around, reading newspapers and the bulletin board. Jones vaulted one lying on the steps and pushed through into the heavy monoxide of midday Des Moines. The building across the street was nearly identical, the entranceway deserted except for two ragged rubber ferns in pots. He made his way across, dancing through traffic to the tune of many horns.

There will be time. Time to catch her before she escapes. Explain it all in lucid terms and spend a day of romantic reunion. Replaying certain inspiring scenes. Fortissimo trombono erecto. Lily, be there or hope is gone.

He rushed into an empty lobby. Not a female to be seen. Except a young lady in thin steel glasses poised and official behind the desk. As Jones clomped across the lobby, her eyes widened and moved quickly down to something on the desk. There was fear behind the thick lenses. He saw himself in a mirror and understood. Three days of beard and hair poking up crazily. A pallor on the skin; eyes dark, sagging, rimmed in red. Worse than the harmless boys in the lobby across the street.

"Miss—"

"Yes? Can I assist you?"

"Miss Robertson. Has she left?"

"She has, sir. Her cab left two or three minutes ago."

"Thank you, miss."

140

"She asked me not to tell you. But I can't willingly deceive anyone."

"That would be a venial sin."

"It would, sir."

"No need wasting our time with the little ones."

"Or the big ones."

"Any, for that matter."

"Quite right, sir. Are you acquainted with the *Christian Weekly?*"

But Jones was out the door, hailing a taxi. Four went by without stopping. Jones cursed them all. Finally a Vets pulled to the curb. He opened the door and flopped in the back seat. The cabbie turned slowly to him.

"You call for a cab?"

"Of course I did. I wasn't waving my arms for the exercise. Aren't you guys supposed to pick up people and take them places?"

"Yeah. That's right. But you gotta phone. Dispatch sets up the customers. We just follow orders."

"Just get me to the train station. Fast as you can go."

"Sorry, bud. I got a customer to pick up."

"I'm your customer. It's an emergency."

"Can't do it. Now get out. Don't make any trouble."

"Give you five bucks."

"No way. The fare is three."

"On top of the fare."

"Well. Wait a minute and I'll ask this lady. She's going the same place."

"A lady?"

"Right. Called in about fifteen minutes ago."

"Go in and ask her. Tell her I'm a clergyman."

"You ain't a clergyman."

"I may be. How do you know I'm not a priest of the poor?"

141

"All right. I'll tell her."

He went in and in a moment emerged with two bags and a hatbox. Jones ducked low in the seat. The car door opened and a large lady slid in beside.

"Hello, Lil."

Shocked eyes looked up and instantly turned away. "Fielding. Leave me alone. Driver!"

"Lil, wait. Let me talk."

She slipped from his grasping hand and out the door.

"Hey, what is it lady? He insult you or something?"

"He's no clergyman. Please put him out or I'll phone your company."

"Hey, lady, I'm sorry. I'll get rid of the bum."

"Lily! I've been cleared," shouting through the dirty back window.

The driver humped to Jones's door and threw it open. "All right, ace. Outta here or I'll wipe up the street with you."

"Listen, driver—"

"No guff or I'll cream you. The lady says out."

"She's my fiancee."

"All the more reason to cream you, you bum."

Jones suddenly noted his arm being wrenched from the socket and his humanity being rudely violated. He struggled and then went limp, the strength gone out. Herded up against a brick wall, he watched Lily enter the cab without looking, settle forward with her face in her hands.

And suddenly very old. Seeing me like this. She looked once and screamed. Fantasies born under cover of night die in the sun. I am a cold December day. All winds and chills and blustering. December and May I know about and stand forewarned.

"Lil! Wait! I've been cleared! Listen Lil!"

But the cab was gone before he could hear whether

142

she'd replied. Out in the street with waving arms. I'll get a bloody driver this time or die trying. A Yellow cab swerved to get around him, but he ran in front and forced it to a halt. He was in and yelling before the driver could turn to see.

"Follow that car! This is life or death!"

The driver looked at him with bland eyes and a small, twitching moustache. "You think this is a Bogart movie or something? You think I can go racing through town like this was Indianapolis?"

"Three bucks says you can."

"I might get a ticket."

"I'll pay half."

"Or lose my job."

"Three-fifty, for God's sake. Just go. It's already out of sight."

"Where's it going?"

"Train station."

"All right, I'll take you. But don't expect me to speed. I got a perfect driving record."

"That's wonderful."

"A man has to keep up certain standards."

"Right. Let's go."

"I'll do the driving if you don't mind. I never force my way into traffic. An opening will come. I may get you there a few minutes later, but I'll get you there safely."

"You'll also get me there cheaply."

"The money don't matter to me where driving safety is concerned. Some guys risk their lives for a few bucks. Not me. You ever hear the story of the turtle and the rabbit?"

"My God forsaketh me."

"Well, you see, this rabbit . . ."

Jones sighed and closed his eyes. With two fingers he

picked foam rubber from a slice in the seat. A pile grew on the floor. When at last they edged out into traffic, he found himself nearly asleep.

"And so that's sort of my motto, see. Slow and steady wins the race every time. In the long run, that is. I just won't go following cars for people, no matter what they say in the movies. I got a wife and kid at home. When the kid gets old enough to drive, he'll learn my motto or get kicked in the ass. I get serious when it comes to safety. You hear me?"

"Now I lay me down to sleep—"

"I'll get there in time."

"Slowly and steadily."

"Right. You're a weird guy."

"Wake me if we get there."

"Whatta you mean 'if'?"

"Good night."

"Jeez. They get weirder every day."

As they yielded for every right of way and stopped for every stop sign, Jones considered the quality of his future. DeJong would have his neck, no doubt. The Dean was right about personal appearances. DeJong was most right-eously indignant behind the back. End of a budding career in sight. Have to sell the house and find some means of simplifying the price of existence. Mother will be horrified at my follies, as always. God. Other lives be lead. Travel light and loose and in thy heart be free. Easier said than done, though. Bold and youthful exhortations, those.

At the train station Jones, clinging to a shred of hope, had the driver wait and dashed inside. At the counter more indifference, hesitation, wasted time.

"Listen, old man, do you wait on people or stand around cracking your jaw?"

"What do you want?"

"Train for Chicago—"

"Pulling out right now."

Jones burst through a turnstile and startled a porter snoozing against a baggage cart.

"Hey, man, you can't—"

Alongside the train like Bumstead after his bus. Leaping, waving into windows. People waving back with grins, guffaws for the crazy man. Look ma. Two cars attacked and no Lily to be seen. Hiding in the can, perhaps, where she found me. Strange how one remembers little flaws like noisy piddling. Forever after when I think of Lil I'll think of that. And petit mal. And better things. Dear human girl, where are you?

The train slowly gained momentum, woofing and wheezing, moving out through a jungle of warehouses and dirty glass. Jones backed away, repressing an impulse to leap aboard and take the car apart. He turned to the station and watched pigeons burst skyward from the tile roof, leaving little heaps of droppings which the rain could never quite scour out. The station, creature of an earlier time, its occasional train passing in and out and pigeons staining its roof, waiting for the crowds which yearly diminished: a quaint symbolism, Jones. Titillates an aging thinkologist to self-examination. But not too deep. Avoid the circumstances of reproach.

He found the locker and removed his suitcase and trombone, quickly checking for a note, finding nothing. Not even her scent on his underwear. Not a trace that she'd even folded things with reverence. He lifted a pair of wrinkled shorts and pushed into a men's room. The reek of urine and suspended Pine Sol nearly leveled him. He clutched a metal door and found his way into a stall. Leaning on a stool, he removed his trousers and shook out the shorts with the infamous dorsal message. Raising them to

145

the light to gauge the quantity and quality of soil, he noticed another inscription penned along the center seam in neat little letters:

> *I gave you everything, but you gave me more.*
> *For a moment, Fielding, it was the loveliest time.*

Ecstatic and hopeless romance on the seat of my shorts. Right through all the faded residue collected there. Something to remember me by, Lily. Something as human as the memories you've left with me. I missed you by an instant, and now I've nothing but the road ahead—what I had before, which now seems to diminish in promise.

18

All the hours. Seven of another sunless day, and Jones bought a chicken and shared it with Ezekiel, who dug out the communion wine and told a hundred true YMCA stories. They tossed the bones in Ezekiel's hat for future reference. Across the way chimneys and skylights stuck the clouds. So many dismal windows. Which was hers? That facade of ugly orange bricks so important now that she had been within them. And was gone. On the roof he noticed a little shingled house with a metal door. It suddenly opened; his heart leaped. A young woman came out with a pail of something, which she emptied on the roof. She paused a moment to inhale a cigarette. Looking at the sky, she blew a lung of smoke out. It caught the wind and disappeared, and then she bent and hiked her skirt to fix a stocking.

"Who's that, Ezekiel?"

"Lucy on the roof."

"Lucy on the roof?"

"That's what the boys call her. She fixes her stocking three times a week. Aren't those fine legs? There are dandy, prancing fellows here who don't appreciate her, but most of us do. I'm eighty and I still do."

"That's inspirational."

"A man loses his sex powers and he might as well be dead."

"Amen. Who is she?"

"A maid at the YW. But she isn't what you'd call a Christian lady."

"She seems charitable enough."

"She doesn't mind giving of herself. She doesn't mind receiving in return, either."

"I think the eyes of God are looking at us."

"Nowhere in this room where they aren't. I'd guess God doesn't mind Lucy. She's an angel of mercy, in a way. She isn't mean or wifey. She's got a big heart and it's always in her work."

"Ask her over."

"Not allowed. We have to go to Lucy's place."

"Too bad."

"Want to pay a visit?"

"Maybe tomorrow."

"I go tomorrow."

"You do?"

"That's right. Once a week is all I manage anymore."

"You have a very healthy religious attitude, if you don't mind me saying so."

"Have some more communion wine. I have plenty in the cellar. You understand I only give it to fellows who need it."

"Decent of you."

Jones got off his chair and sprawled on the floor among

148

the saints and angels. Ezekiel filled a jelly jar to the brim and handed it down to him. Jones lifted the glass with an eye to the old man.

"Here's to a happy man. To you, Ezekiel, and the secrets you've discovered."

"And to you, Mr. Jones, for some of what I have. And there's lots to spare since I got right with the Lord. You get right with the Lord and you'll feel it too."

Glasses rose and clicked. Through the wine Ezekiel's eyes gleamed like rain on roses.

"And to Lucy on the roof, Ezekiel. May her generous exposures never invite influenza or the law."

Jones set his jar down beside Gabriel trumpeting. He lay back and yawned. God's orange eyes peered at him, big, heavy cat's eyes burning. A mute, inglorious William Blake drinking wine beside him. Gulley Jimson painted feet on walls, but never God's eyes above his bed.

"Oh!"

Ezekiel started, wine spilling through whiskers and staining his green porter's coat. "My heart."

Jones struggled to his feet, upending several saints. "Oh boy."

"Hey, Mr. Jones."

"Oh boy. The end is in sight. What's the time, Ezekiel?"

"Eight twenty-five. What's the matter?"

"Five minutes. I might make it. Ezekiel, how do I look? I have to make a speech tonight."

"A speech? You shouldn't give a speech looking like that. Who are you giving a speech to?"

"Girl Guides of America. At the Rudolph. Well done, Jones. Well done. Consistent blundering from start to stop."

"Shave, Mr. Jones. You aren't fit for calling hogs."

"No time, Ezekiel. It's my ass if I don't go now."

149

"Slow down. I've never seen a man in such a hurry all the time. You take my Sunday coat and hat. Here. In the closet. Put them on and don't take them off. Tell folks you've got the turtle fever."

"Forget it, Ezekiel. Take two of you to make one of me."

"I can get two of me in my Sunday coat. I buy them big."

"All right. They take me pot luck."

Ezekiel dragged out a decrepit houndstooth overcoat with huge padded shoulders and a richness of mothballs and body scents. Also a shiny black derby hat.

"Perfect, Ezekiel. Perfect. This coat keeps the ankles warm. Put me in it. I'll be smashing."

"The Army doesn't often have coats as long as this. The Lord smiled on me that day."

"Pray He smiles on me tonight."

"It's made for you, Mr. Jones. Try the hat. Too small. That's a shame. You have a big head."

"The hat is perfect. Farewell. No time to admire myself. I'll return these safely."

"Sure."

"Only three minutes now."

And Jones hit the street before one was up. Sailing along Sterling, buttoning as he went, he felt the wine begin to glow with the crisp air on his face. He fought an urge to put out his arms and soar like a B-29. Uncle Dummy, the old black, green-bearded broommaker down the road from College of the Pines, soared on the streets and said he was Icarus, arms full out and dipping winds, and people turning into shops to avoid him. There was a man with an answer. Jones accelerated through garbage cans set out on the curb, saw a grapefruit full of egg shells and booted it under a bus. He raised his arms and felt the sudden uplift of air as his feet left the sidewalk and ears popped from heights of spirit.

150

"Hey, you crazy ass. Whatta you think you are, a duck or something? Knock me over and I'll smash your ass."

"Flying north. Bless you, sir."

"Must be a full moon tonight."

"Quack, quack, quack."

"Wow. A psycho."

Patrons of Chill's looked up from the bar as the great craft passed at six feet, cruising low. He buzzed a little knot of kids looking at dirty books through a cigar store window. They watched silently. Up the street the Rudolph's thousand windows beckoned. He flew under the awning and into the lobby, landing neatly, with sound effects, at the main desk.

"Pilot to crew. Now hear this."

"Hey, sport. You aren't really welcome here anymore. Get lost or I'll call the captain."

"I have a speaking engagement to keep tonight. The Grand Assembly of Girl Guides has requested my presence at their banquet."

"Come off it. You look like a bum."

"These garments are props for my speech. I have hidden beneath them a fully accoutremented Girl Guide uniform. If you insist on disputing my word, you may phone up Miss Grinelda Fullpot for verification."

"One second. Don't pull any fast ones."

"Roger."

He retreated to the office as Jones hummed a march and tipped a hat to Archie. Who rumbled toward him.

"Stop, you. No violence. It preys upon its perpetrator and gets him in the end. Such are the laws of life."

"Up your ass."

"I'll pretend I didn't hear that for the sake of your job."

"My job is busting asses of bums like you."

He reached out, but Jones eluded him.

"Archie! It's all right. Sport here is speaking in the Embassy Room tonight. Right down the hall, Mr. Jones. Miss Fullpot says they're waiting for you."

"Sorry, old boy. There'll be others to crush and mangle. There always are."

Archie grunted sullenly and walked away.

Close, Jones. Near shipwreck before the storm has even hit. Embassy Room it is. Fly down this corridor gritting the teeth. Preparing faces for those we meet. And words of wisdom unminced and undiluted. Something to get them. And thyself off the hook. Before me in gold scroll the fatal words, the torture chamber, which I must make a heaven of.

Bursting in on the august gathering. Heavy doors boomed and echoed. Ladies looked with uncertain eyes at the mighty figure framed in the doorway, then at each other; a nervous prodding of jello and lettuce leaves commenced. Never before had he viewed so many uniformed and embroidered women at once. A nice Nazi flavor to the Embassy Room. One must proceed with a guarded grip on the testicles.

Out of the quivering leaves and fluttering lashes, a voice resounded firm and sure as a steamship whistle.

"Mr. Jones! I have a place here for you at the head table. I assume you will want to make your little speech and leave. We have important business to attend to tonight."

"Miss Fullpot. It is a pleasure to be in your company once again."

"You can dispense with the pleasant stuff, Mr. Jones. I'm not pleased with your company. I allowed you this opportunity only because these ladies insisted. I, personally, would have preferred to let the courts handle the matter."

"I bow to your generosity, ladies. What are we eating?"

"*You* aren't eating. Make your speech and go."

A bewhiskered crone at the head table took her arm. "Please, Grinelda. The man is obviously down and out. Let me at least put some biscuits in a little bag."

"I love biscuits, Miss Fullpot. My granny fed me them when I was just a little whiffet."

"Please, dear. I'll go to the kitchen and fix him a sack lunch. We need to help such creatures, not scorn them."

"All right, mother. But you are generous to a fault. This man deserves any punishment we can deal out."

"His presence here is punishment enough. Don't you feel that way, girls?"

A few righteous nods.

"You are too kind, good ladies. You are worthy of the name of your honorable occupation. May I take my place at the podium, Miss Wombat?"

"It's Wolpot. Don't you make fun of me. I won't have it."

"Forgive me, Miss Wolpot. May I speak?"

"Right here. And be quick. You've already wasted too many precious minutes."

Jones strode to her side, helped her into a chair, and snatched an olive from her plate.

"You put that—"

"Haven't eaten for days. Not for days. Confessions of this sort are quite debilitating."

"Get on with it."

"Thank you. Ladies. Ladies of this Grand Assembly of the Girl Guides of America. Ladies and Miss Chairman, Grinelda C. Wolpot, I welcome you here as guests of Des Moines' most exclusive dining, sleeping, watering, and bilking establishment. I have come tonight to attempt to make amends for alleged indecencies committed against the innocent eyes of Miss Wolpot and several of her foundlings who came upon me in an unfortunate moment in the city woods." Jones lifted a celery stick from Grinelda's plate and shied it at the audience. "Before I proceed with so painful a task, I would like to examine some of the facets of contemporary morality and consider, if I may, their relationship to the novels of James Fenimore Condom, who is so important to us of Anglo-Saxon tradition."

"Jones, you get to the point or the deal is off."

A murmur began, rose, then became a single voice. "Let him speak, Grinelda. It's impolite to keep interrupting."

Grinelda paled, reddened, rapped her plate with a fork.

"I am the chairman of this meeting. I insist that he get to the point."

"If I am allowed to continue, you may see that all my comments are properly coherent and of a single intent."

Across the aisle someone whispered, "Who is he?"

"Continue, Mr. Jones!"

"There goes in the world a belief, unsupported by a single Biblical passage, that woman is a kind of sacred cow, a cow to be protected, honored, courted, and occasionally made love to by the male of the species. If you be a woman, as most of you be, you may find such treatment offensive and generally distracting. Do you agree, Miss Wolpot."

"What of it?"

"The female of the species deserves equal treatment, equal rights, equal status to the male. She is offended by the label 'weaker sex' and works to overcome such dated and stereotyped thinking. Correct, Mr. Chairman?"

"Men are fools. I take care of myself."

"That's because you are liberated, Miss Wolpot. You function in every way as successfully as a man."

"I do, I'm happy to say."

"And should be, Grinelda. I'm not making jokes."

"Then get to the point."

154

"Have you ever known a man to turn in a woman for indecent exposure?"

Grinelda paused. And paused.

"What about James Fenimore Condom? You aren't making sense."

"James Fenimore Condom? Oh, yes. Yes, yes. You see, he was once arrested on a trumped-up charge of indecent exposure and spent the better portion of his middle age in a prison on the Glimmerglass. Seems some woman, some perverse Puritan, watching with a telescope, glimpsed him running from barn to house in only a lace dickey. The poor man had removed his clothes when he thought them contaminated with . . . with . . . *the hoof and mouth,* which had raged in epidemic proportions through his cattle and his daughters. My situation is obviously analogous."

"You'll be sorry."

"Yes, probably. I'm sorry you peeked. It no doubt was painful for you. But I also was beset by ailments that I had no control over. Ladies, I would not for the life of me knowingly show Miss Wolpot my private organs. The little girls I am remorseful about. But I must say they responded to the situation more rationally than Miss Wolpot did."

Outside the windows a garbage truck whined, gobbling up empty bottles. Grinelda gripped a fork as if preparing to drive it into his bowels.

"Your attack on me, Miss Wolpot, was premeditated and uncharitable. For all I know it was sexually motivated."

"Oh!"

"—but that is only conjecture. I chose to give you the benefit of the doubt and not press charges. And what did you do in return?"

"You, sir, are dismissed from this meeting. Leave or I'll

155

have the bell captain remove you. You'll regret this, I guarantee it."

"Grinelda. Please wait. Here is your lunch, Mr. Jones. There is a chicken breast in there, too. Thank you for coming. It took a great deal of courage to face my daughter."

"Mother!"

"Leave the man alone, Grinelda. He has apologized to us."

"That was no apology!"

"It most certainly was. If I'd met Mr. Jones in the woods, I'd have acted with more compassion."

Jones tapped a thumbnail on a tooth. "I'm sure you would have, mother."

"Don't you call her mother! She's my mother!"

"Your father had a weak bladder, too, Grinelda."

"Kidney, my dear."

"Oh. I beg your pardon, Mr. Jones."

Setting her chin, Grinelda quelled the storms in her cheeks and grew calm. "Mother, be quiet and sit down. Mr. Jones, we've had about all of you we can stand. Please leave. You'll be hearing from Lieutenant Sullivan."

"Have I been pardoned?"

Miss Wolpot squelched all opposition with a booming "Go! The Lieutenant will let you know everything you need know. I have nothing more to say to you."

"But you said—"

"Good-bye!"

"All right. Au revoir, Miss Wolpot. Ladies. And especially you, mother."

"The chicken needs salt, Mr. Jones."

"Thank you, dear."

"Come again, won't you?"

"I'm not sure."

"Will that be all right, Grinelda?"

"Mr. Jones will not be welcome here again. Sit down, mother. Leave, Jones. Not another word."

"I'm leaving now without another word."

"Be quick about it."

"Quick as a flash, ladies. Jones is here—and gone."

And out on the street he found a sky alight with dazzling stars. As he walked, teen-agers labored at their fumy courtships car to car.

Wonder if Lily has ever danced the lindy. Or heard of it. When the urges die, what would we have talked about? It's better. God has His plans. Grinelda, too. And I don't know which I fear the most.

19

Oil and steam and metallic smells. A partial apple lay dehydrating in the ashtray at his side. Sweet decay. Jones sat silent, shaven, a large striped Windsor knot snug against his throat. He'd pressed his two bags into the wooden seat beside him. The trombone case, bell end down, stood balanced between his knees. It was late afternoon in the train station; his eyes moved lazily, his mind afloat in the heavy warmth of sun through the windows. A freight train clattered through without stopping. He thought of jumping it. The luxury of an empty boxcar, no eyes, no gnashing of teeth. No swill bucket for a seat.

The train to Denver was full; Jones was on standby again. Without luck, he would enjoy Des Moines for another twelve hours. A sleepy gloom settled in, took hold. He'd sit there, unmoving, all the hours. Long as it took. The Des Moines disaster. Good name for squalid novel. No more venturing out in this town. Every step was a risk.

159

"Dr. Jones! Hey, I don't believe it. This is too cool. Whoever thought I'd see you here?"

Jones closed his eyes, feigning sleep, cursing the forces of circumstance, fate, God, and the oracle of Apollo. He didn't recognize the voice, but the salutation was unmistakable: some wretched former student up out of the woodwork, dashing the luxury of anonymity.

"Hey, Dr. Jones. It's me."

Jones forced one eyelid up, saw two fringed deerskin boots and the ragged cuffs of blue jeans.

"So it is."

"Hey, look, it's me, Grooters."

His eyes moved reluctantly upward; his mind sorted through pages of old gradebooks. Grooters. Grooters. Howard Grooters. Through a sparse, wispy red beard he recognized the beefy, vapid face, the crinkly little eyes.

"Hello, Howard."

"Wow. That's wild. You remember me."

"That's right."

"I didn't think you would. I wasn't the greatest student back in those days."

"Those days?"

"Yeah, I've changed a lot in two years. No more frat rat Grooters, as you can see. I guess you could call me a semi-freak. I'm grooving out to Frisco to see what's happening. My old man tossed me out because of the beard. It's the best thing that ever happened to me, besides pot, Doc."

"I'm happy for you, Howard."

"Hey, Doc, what are you doing in this four-square town?"

"I'm running from the law."

"Hey, man. Heavy. Is that the truth?"

"I'm waiting for a train to Denver."

"Yeah. That's what I thought. It would blow their minds

160

at the Pines if you were, though. I'm just passing through myself. I'm waiting for my cousin. He was supposed to tell off his old man, too, and then groove out with me. Guess he isn't going to show, though. He's too straight a guy. I figured he'd flake out on me, so I'm not too disappointed."

"Wonderful."

"I mean, I didn't dig this guy much. But he's family. Hey! Wow! Listen, I just got a terrific idea. I'm going through Denver. Why don't you ride along?"

"No thank you. I have a train ticket."

"They'll refund it, Doc. Hey, come on. We'll have a gas. Save you some money. And me too if you help me with a few expenses."

"I'd rather not. It's kind of you."

"Hey, that ticket says standby. Why didn't you say so? You might wait here all night."

Jones cursed silently, and shoved the ticket in his pocket.

"I'll ask the guy what your chances are. Just a minute."

And he was off before Jones could arrange his tongue around an objection. Howard Grooters. Rather have the mange than his company. The prospective savings were not worth the psychic cost of fifteen hours with Howard.

"Hey, Doc, this dude says chances are you'll be here all night. Four standbys ahead of you, see. You're coming with me. I'm driving all night. Right through. We'll be there before you're on this train."

"Thank you, Howard, I believe I'll wait."

"The guy says he'll refund your ticket."

"He did?"

"Sure. C'mon. We've got lots of heavy stuff to rap about. I've been reading Rod McKuen. Wow. You know him, Doc? He blows my mind—"

"Howard. I've been very sick the last few days. I'm

afraid what conversation I might maintain would be low-key. In fact, you might find me sleeping most of the way. Would that bother you?"

"Bother me? I'll just listen to you snore. If you snore as well as you lecture, I'll be happy."

"All right, Howard. You may carry my bags."

"Cool, Doc. It's my pleasure."

Jones cashed in $36.50 worth of ticket and followed Howard to the parking lot. Into the fat sponginess of a mint-green GTO convertible with dashboard gleaming chrome knobs and dials for RPM, pulse, and blood pressure. Howard filled the trunk and slid in beside him.

"Some beast, eh Doc?"

"How do you afford a car like this?"

"My old man bought it. He did a few right things in his life. I don't hate him or anything. Hey, wow, that reminds me. He told me about your wife dying. I was sorry to hear that. Such a young chick, I mean."

Jones nodded and Howard exploded from the lot, shooting pea gravel into the grills of a half-dozen cars. Around a corner, tires screaming objections, and up a ramp to the superhighway; Howard merged without a backward glance and made haste to catch the leaders.

"Three hundred fifty cubes," he mumbled, eyes huge and glistening.

"Howard. Do you generally drive like this?"

"You bet, Doc. Wow, yeah. This is a sweet green beast."

"I'm getting out."

"What? Hey wait. Shut that door, for Jesus Christ's sake. We're doing eighty-five."

"Stop this car, Howard."

"Easy, Doc, easy. I'll slow it down. Wow, I didn't think you'd mind a little guts."

"I hate guts."

162

"Jeez, Doc."

"No wonder you flunked out of college, paying upkeep on this weapon. What you need is a good forty-dollar car."

"Yeah. That's rich. Chicks dig a forty-dollar car. You're asking me to cut off one of my nuts."

"A nineteen sixty-two Rambler would be good for your character, Howard. And your health."

"Right on, Doc."

"Sixty-five. Any higher and I'll jump."

"Okay. I can stand it. Crawl in the back and sack out if you want. Maybe you'll feel better after a few Zs."

"I feel fine. What's the matter? Do I sound sick?"

"A little."

"Well. I just got out of the hospital."

"Yeah? In this town? You must have been sick."

"I'll try the back."

"Be my guest. There's a blanket on the floor. Mind if I turn the radio on?"

"It's your car, Howard."

"Sweet dreams, Doc. You dig acid rock?"

"Love it, Howard."

"Cool. Listen."

One hundred decibels of amplified organ pounded from a rear speaker. Guitars screaming like some Dantesque hell-bound soul. Right on, Jones. Groove with them. What's the trouble. Use the blanket as a muffler about the ears. Howard's head bobbing about like an apple in a tub. Fingers snapping out cadence. They're singing about the caverns of your mind, Howard. Where the wind howls through. When you sat by your window in the back row I could hear it clearly. That hollow place. Cavernous. God, I'm old.

Jones slept fitfully, awoke freezing, with someone thumping his leg just below the buttocks.

"Move over man. You got company."

"Who goes there?" The moon curved in a corner of the windshield.

"Two cold freaks. Move over. Share the wealth. You don't need all that blanket."

Beside him hunched a small, grinning girl in a ratty fur coat with a bedroll slung over one shoulder. A strange explosion of long, frizz-curled hair all but smothered her. Little eyes peered out. Lips a bit scummy at the corners where hairs caught when she talked, face a little gray and sick. From hair balls, maybe.

"Make room, Doc. We've got a couple more going with us."

A young man in front turned and offered his hand. It was Abe Lincoln, stovepipe hat, wart, and all.

"Call me Honest Abe."

"I was about to."

"This chick is Chrysanthemum."

"Hello, Chrysanthemum."

"Pleased to meet you. I didn't mean to cop your blanket. Just share it."

"Be my guest. Why is it so cold in here, Howard?"

"Had the top down while you were sleeping, Doc. I dig the air in my hair."

Chrysanthemum huddled under fuzz and fur and Jones's blanket. "I dig the heat on my feet."

"If heat's your thing, Chris, I got all you need."

Honest Abe placed a thin white hand on Howard's shoulder. "Her name is Chrysanthemum. You can call me just plain Honest."

"I dig, Honest. Chrysanthemum. Too cool. Wow."

"Howard."

"Yeah, Doc."

"Wow is an expletive that one should use sparingly. Save

164

it for moments of transcendent ecstasy. Overuse dulls the effect."

Chrysanthemum leaned against Jones and stared into his eyes. "Heavy. Who are you?"

"Hey," Howard shouted above the heater's tempest. "Meet my ex-English prof, Dr. Fielding Jones. I ran into him in dismal Des Moines. He's the coolest teacher I ever had."

"I flunked you, Howard."

Honest sent a stern, cold look his way. "Hey. Bad. Nobody should flunk."

"You underestimate Howard."

"Yeah, Honest, it's true. I was pretty stupid back then. I deserved it. Hey, wow, do you know what he did in class one day? I mean, right in front of the whole bunch of us?"

"Tell us." Chrysanthemum edged up on Jones.

"You tell them, Doc."

"I've forgotten, Howard. You do the honors. It's difficult to keep a tally of my misbehavior."

"Well, Doc was doing some pretty dull stuff, see. Emerson or somebody."

Honest glared at Howard. "Emerson is a genius."

Jones felt a diminutive glow around the area of his left lung. "Did I hear you right, young man?"

"Emerson and Thoreau were true mystics. Western Orientals. I burn incense in their honor."

Howard continued: "I mean, that was back in my stupid days, dig? Nobody had read the stuff and some of us were still half gone for a beer bust the night before. Doc was doing all the work, and us digging nothing. All of a sudden he slams his book shut and heaves it right out the window. No shit. Right out the goddam window, dig? And here we are on the seventh floor. Then you know what he does?

165

He starts taking off his clothes. First his coat, then his tie, then his shirt and his undershirt. And his shoes and socks. When he starts going for his belt we all panic because this is John Calvin's college, dig? A very holy place. Then he stops with the belt and puffs his big chest out and says 'All right, we're going to prepare the body for the mind,' or something like that, and he has us do calisthenics for the rest of the hour. I mean, wow. It blew our minds. He led us in deep knee bends and everything else. I'll never forget it."

Honest watched Jones; Chrysanthemum took his arm, gripped it to her breasts. Everything else so small but these.

"I would have done the same thing," Honest said. "I agree that the body must be prepared before any true vision can be achieved."

"Honest wouldn't stop at the pants, though. God, I would dig a father like you, Doc. Except I'd want to ball you all the time. That's bad with your dad."

"Chrysanthemum has a father hang-up. He's a professional killer in Vietnam. So I become the father figure or anyone handy."

"Were you in a war, Doc?" Chrysanthemum held him fiercely.

"I was a soldier of sorts."

"Did you kill babies?"

"I killed nothing. Except bottles. Many many bottles. I pretended I was blind for two months, and the war ended before I could be shipped out. That's my tale of valor."

"Oh, cool! Beautiful! I love you, Doc! Isn't he beautiful, Honest? Wow!"

"He seems to be a man of integrity."

"Howard gave the wheel a hardy slap. "Hey, didn't I tell you he was cool? *Didn't I?*"

166

Jones blinked and looked at the moon, a small cold slice. A dim aura of sun still glowed on the horizon, and in the half light he could see dark, flat, fenceless fields, uninhabited earth from horizon to horizon.

"Howard! Stop the car!"

"God, Doc, what's the matter? This is no place to take a leak."

"Look! Outside! Stop, Howard!"

Panicked, Howard swerved onto the shoulder too quickly and spun in a circle, tossing rocks, coming to rest on the edge of an irrigation ditch.

Jones jumped out into a plowed field. Honest threw open the door, crying "Dig it! Dig it! A spin-out! Let's do it again!"

"Look!" Jones shouted, turning a full circle.

"What the hell is it, Doc. Jesus, you scared the hell out of me."

"Look, Howard. All of you. Look around you. What do you see?"

Honest scanned the horizons, eyes growing large. "God! Wow! I see it! Here, Chrysanthemum. Blow your mind!"

Creeping out cautiously, Howard and Chrysanthemum searched with frightened eyes. Suddenly she beamed and threw her pack down.

"Oh, wow! Oh, wow!"

"What the hell is it?" Howard shouted. "Goddammit, I don't see anything you guys."

"Look, man, can't you see? We're on the moon!"

"Jeez, Honest. This is Nebraska. Did you guys have some speed while I wasn't looking? Shit. My car is all scratched up."

"Howard. Follow the horizon. What do you see?"

Howard took a quick turn around. "Nothing."

"That's right. A hundred miles in every direction. No

houses, no fences, no telephone poles, no power lines, no people. Just this highway, that car, and us. We're the only people on earth!"

"Dig it!" Honest shouting, tossing his stovepipe hat into the air.

"Beautiful, beautiful! Let's have a joint, Honest!"

"Later, baby. This trip is natural."

"It's the West." Jones held up an arm.

"Let's get outta here," Howard cried.

"It's the new world. Like stout Cortez upon a peak in Darien. The uncorrupted earth. My God, I feel it. The Golden Age. Grasses born without seed. I'm Adam. You're Eve," pointing to Chrysanthemum.

"Crazy! Let's take off our clothes!"

"I am Abel. Honest Abel."

Howard looking puzzled and vaguely contemptuous. "Wow. You really save the good part for me."

"Cheer up, Howard." Jones wrapped an arm about his shoulders and led him out into the mud of new-turned earth. "Feel it stick to the shoes, Howard. It's rich, packed with vitality. It's the mother of us all."

"My carpets are screwed."

"I know how they felt, Howard. Those Dutch sailors discovering Long Island. The Swedes finding the plains. All those years of teaching and I never really understood."

"Cool, Doc. This place spooks me. Let's move out. No place to hide here."

"Howard, you're a Calvinist."

"Where could you neck? Not even a cornstalk to hide behind."

"There's no one here to hide from but God, Howard."

"That's what I mean. It's like standing around naked."

"Let's!" Chrysanthemum tossed off her coat and began unbuttoning her blouse.

168

"We better get back in the car," Howard said.

"Button up. You'll freeze your tits tonight."

"Aw, Honest."

"Wait till Denver. It's warmer there."

"Don't stop on account of me," Howard said.

"I guess I better."

"Well, don't on account of me."

"Howard, you're leering."

"Well, jeez, if he wants to see I don't mind. They're my tits."

"Me? Not me. Don't do it on my account."

"Come on, Chrysanthemum. Get to the farm and you can let it all hang out."

Jones watched her button up. Honest shut her coat and secured it.

"What farm in Denver?"

"Snakegrass Farm."

"That's a coincidence. My son works there."

"Yeah? Wow. That's wild. Does he dig it?"

"I don't know. He's never said much about it. I don't even know what he raises there. Charles is the weak, silent type. I have difficulty imagining him milking a cow. He was never much of a physical being."

Honest pointed to the darkening western horizon. "Snakegrass Farm in the morning, baby. We're almost free."

"Wow, Honest. I really feel beautiful. I don't ever want to go back."

"We stay forever if it's good."

Jones tugged an earlobe. "This farm—God, I smell a rat—is it really a farm?"

Honest had grown dim in the fading light. "Well, man, it's no government co-op, if that's what you mean."

"Tell me."

"It's a freak farm, Doc. A commune. You dig?"

"I dig. I sincerely dig."

Howard moved toward the car. "It's dark, you guys. We better go."

"All right, Howard. One more look. Someone trespassing on our road. Charles in a commune. Jesus Jenny."

"Truck," Honest said, as it roared up and by them in a haze of diesel fumes. "Septic tanks."

"Appropriate." Jones nodded.

"Come on, Doc. Let's get out of here. You guys wipe off your feet, okay? Crap, look at all those scratches."

"Hey, man. That bothers you, doesn't it. I mean, that your kid's in a commune."

"Leave him alone, Honest," Chrysanthemum said. "He's just got to get used to it."

"I've just got to get used to it," Jones said. "I've never had a kid in a commune before."

"If I were your kid I'd stay home with you, Doc."

"Thanks, Chrysanthemum."

"And ball you all day long."

"Oh."

"Honest doesn't like me to talk like that."

"It's your bag, baby."

"Honest used to teach Sunday school. Then he met me and got polluted."

"Flatter yourself." Honest tipped his hat low over his eyes as if he'd heard the speech before.

"You two want to fight over me? I'll give my body to the winner."

"I concede," Jones said, climbing into the front beside Howard.

"You big shit. I was defending you."

"Shut up and get in." Honest pushed her into the back seat.

170

"You bastards! You got no balls. Wow, I just terrify the shit out of you guys."

Placing his stockinged feet on Howard's lime dash, Jones instantly stopped all conversation. Windows flew down and Chrysanthemum began to cry stormily. Within seconds she was asleep on Honest's shoulder.

"Jeez, Doc. You took care of her." Howard offered a stick of Juicy Fruit. "Your insides must be screwed to hell."

Jones nodded as he watched a fragile, blinking light navigate the sky. "The fart, Howard, is our truest symbol," he said. "It is the outward manifestation of the inner self. No other tangible measure is quite so accurate."

"A real stench."

"Exactly."

20

May the first. One month to the day since Sarah left. Happy deathday. Wish you could see me now, shooting ropes across the generation gorge. Dreaming open-eyed of the little girl whose golden hair I'd brush after the bath, the girl we never had, and hold her in flannel gowns as I told my tales. Even those rare sweet moments with Charles dance now in my brain. And I am silent beside these sad children, born rich in a waning world. An old man alone, all precious baggage left behind. I wanted you, little Dutch girl, some day before my own leave-taking. But there's no going back now with Charles in a commune committing grandchildren to a public flock.

Dawn of the first May day and Nebraska spreading like a large flat quilt on a bed. Or is it Colorado? Howard suddenly whooped, leaning on the horn, raising them all from semisleep.

"Please, Howard."

"Sorry, Doc. We're in Colorado. The governor just welcomed us. Two hours to Denver. I'm halfway to Frisco. Wow!"

Miles of silence in the back seat. Howard, feeling giddy, pitched off the highway onto a narrow gravel farm road, pulled into a patch of dry thistles, and stopped.

"Anybody mind me putting the top down? I gotta breathe."

"Your car, man." Honest's voice was phlegmy from long silence.

"Wow, he talks." Chrysanthemum sounded wifely.

Jones grunted, raising the collar of his coat. The top whined back as Howard proudly watched.

"Hey, I dig these country roads. Let's try this one a few miles. See if we can find some Indians."

"Good idea, Howard."

And out of the thistles they spun, air in their hair and grit billowing behind, the land dustier now that the soil was officially western. But no sign of mountains out on the edge. Tufted grass and occasional thin cows populated the fields. They passed a farm crawling with dusty pigs. Sign said "Bacon Acres, J. Lemson." Up ahead on three quarters of the road bounced a loaded manure spreader behind a green John Deere.

"Stench!" Honest shouted.

"You again, Doc?" Chrysanthemum leaned over the seat.

"Better put the top up, Howard."

"We'll be by it in a second. No sweat. Hold your breath."

Howard roared up to within several inches as clots of dung and straw bounced to the road with regularity.

"Son of a bitch won't move over."

"Give him a moment, Howard. The road will widen."

"Get your ass off the road!" Howard shouted, raising a

174

fist. The farmer glanced back with a sleepy look. "Goddam redneck! Get over or I'll run you in a ditch!"

The farmer's face remained calm; apparently he couldn't hear above the roar of his machinery. So Howard leaned on the horn.

"I wish you would reconsider what you're doing, Howard."

"That bastard isn't going to move."

"Try a smile."

"Sure thing, Doc." Howard raised his middle finger. The farmer caught it, grinned, and reached back toward the spreader.

"That got him," Howard said.

Suddenly, his beefy face disappeared. He screamed something and swiped at his smothered eyes. Jones watched with rare interest. Then something flopped on his own lap.

"Ye-e-e!" Honest yowled.

Jones turned to find him drowning in great steaming piles. Lime upholstery quickly turned rusty brown and spiked straw. Jones's right ear was suddenly filled.

"I'm blind! I'm blind!" Howard panicked, accelerating up under the grinding spreader. Jones dropped to the floor, finding the brakes with his hands, fighting the thick red ankles back.

"Howard! You'll kill us all! Hit the brakes!"

The large fringed foot responded, pinning Jones's fingers to the pedal. He lay silently screaming, but safe from attack. Chrysanthemum shrieked from the back seat floor as the storm pummeled them. Honest's stovepipe hat blew over the back of the car and down the road. The stench was heady, overpowering. Jones, resigned to pain, found massive theological questions being resolved with sudden ease. There was no hell Milton could conceive that outdid

175

existence. No greater degradation than enduring this day to day.

They stopped and dust billowed up and covered them. Jones pulled his fingers from beneath Howard's foot and sat up. Honest and Chrysanthemum slowly rose from the floor. No one spoke. Howard struck the wheel once and began to weep. Cow pie caked his eyelashes. Up ahead the John Deere turned from the road and set off cross-country, the spreader still flinging its cargo.

"Howard. There was a stream back a mile or so. Maybe we could clean up."

Wordlessly, Howard turned the car and retreated.

Jones stood in his shorts in six inches of freezing, muddy water in a culvert beneath the road, waiting for Chrysanthemum to finish with the soap. Honest, all hair and bones, combed his beard with four fingers. Jones watched the rise and fall of Chrysanthemum's astounding breasts as she clawed soap into her hair. Nipples large as jar tops, enough to feed an orphanage, unhesitatingly revealed to anyone interested. Except Howard, who guarded the car, wiping it out with long dry grass, awaiting his separate moment in the culvert. But no desire prickling in anyone's blood. Chrysanthemum handed him the soap and watched as he began scrubbing out his right ear.

"Hey, Doc. Those shorts turn me on."

"I'm not surprised."

"Leave him alone. Can't you see he doesn't dig it right now? Man, that was the worst scene of my life. It's funny but I can't even laugh."

"I need a smoke, Honest."

"I'll roll two if the stuff's okay. How about you, Doc?"

"No."

Prefer another pain killer. Giant killer, Hemingway

called it. Get it from my case when most of the stench is washed downstream. Share it with no one, even Howard. On the walls of the culvert the scrawls of appropriate obscenities. "Shirley's fine in 69. Call 546–9370." The essence of my life. Backward and downward forever.

They sent their clothing surging downstream, Honest lamenting the loss of the world's one true Lincoln suit. Chrysanthemum went happily bare, drying on Jones's pajamas.

"Hey, thanks, Doc. It's lucky you put this stuff in the trunk. I dig men's pajamas."

"What'll I wear?" Honest asked.

"Take your pick."

"I'll drown in these things. All I can find are white shirts."

"That's all I have."

"I never wore a white shirt before."

"You did too. In Sunday school."

"Come on," Jones said. "Howard wants his turn. I've got to get to Denver. My son is there."

"His son is there, Honest."

"Yeah. Cool."

"He know you're coming, Doc?"

"No."

"Hey, excitement. Is that a gun you've got in that long case?"

"It's a trombone."

"Yeah, I'll bet."

"It is."

"Okay, Doc."

"Shit, lay off, Chrysanthemum."

Jones looked up. Slumped at the top of the culvert in orange underpants, Howard forlornly waited.

21

Howard dropped them on a foothill above Boulder. He hadn't spoken once, even when the mountains had loomed up out of the smoke fifty miles away like great waves rising suddenly in a placid sand sea. Chrysanthemum and Honest huddled by a rock, aswim in Jones's clothes.

"Thank you, Howard. Please accept this money for your trouble."

"Two bucks. Je-sus," pounding the accclerator, Jones barely retrieving his arm and bills as Howard galloped down the mountain in a cloud of gases.

"Did I insult him by offering?"

Honest shrugged, and Chrysanthemum opened the tops of the pajamas, baring half her bazooms to the startled sun. On a granite shelf a painted snake lay coiled and hooded in tall yellow grass. A path began at the shelf and descended into a pine gorge. Jones looked down the road.

179

Boulder lay enshrouded in haze. Barely visible beneath were many neat rows of rectangular dwellings, the sprawl of university buildings and grounds acrawl with creatures; many vehicles trundled forward in lines like processionary caterpillars. Out beyond, Denver smothered in a gray pall.

"Dead people," Honest muttered. "Let's find the farm."

Jones nodded and plunged down through rocks and crevices, gripping branches and crashing through the underbrush with a trombone and two cases beneath the arms. At the bottom of a gorge a girl appeared on a white horse and was gone before he could blink.

"There it is," Honest said. "Down there. Blow my mind."

Then again the horse and the girl, and behind them four small long buildings with tin roofs. A swollen stream rushed through the center of the gorge and several men worked bare-chested in a field. One followed a horse and plow. Smoke rose from a stone chimney which a woman leaned over, stirring something in a pot. Three naked children played beside her.

"You think they'll want us, Honest."

"Sure, baby. They'll want us."

"God, that's Charles behind that plow. My kid doing honest work."

"You sound like my old man, Doc. You really do. *My kid doing honest work.*" Chrysanthemum pointed at him. "You think because he's a freak he can't work? That's real trite, Doc."

Jones moved past her and down the path. My kid. In a field behind a horse. Historical pendulums swinging back. An honester labor than I ever undertook. Preach Thoreau for a dozen years and your kid ends up living it. As I go on my mean and moiling way.

Toting trombone and cases, stumbling down through

180

embracing rocks and cliffs, he edged up on the field. Charles, intent on the earth and yanked along by the horse, didn't see. A huge, bearded John the Baptist with a hoe approached him.

"Call me Ishmael," he boomed, sweat beading in the hair on his massive chest.

"Ishmael who?"

"Schultz. Welcome to the farm. You can help in the fields. We all lived through our first winter. The Great Spirit has blessed us with strength and a beautiful day for planting. Take off your shirt and join your brothers."

"Charles is my son. Would you call him?"

"Charles?"

"The one behind the plow."

"That's Mandrake."

"Mandrake?"

"Yes."

"Would you call Mandrake? I have reason to believe he's my son."

"Are you here to try to take him away?"

"No."

Ishmael nodded to Chrysanthemum and Honest as they approached the woman at the stone fireplace.

"They're staying," Jones said.

"Hey. Stuff. I'll knock off for a while. Try the hoe." Thrusting it into Jones's hand.

"What about Mandrake?"

"Call him yourself. You got a tongue, man."

Jones dropped his hoe and cases in the grass, opened one, and removed a fine nickel-plate trombone which he put to his lips and blew. Charles looked up, blinking several times. He shouted something to the horse and the plow stopped. Moving slowly over through the clods, a faint smile on his lips. Jones feeling embarrassed, an inter-

181

loper, wishing he hadn't blown the horn. Silly and old in his pleated pants and wrinkled shirt. The sun gleamed on Charles's thin brown chest. Rich smells of pine and moist black earth and honest sweat.

"Hello, Fielding," extending a muddy hand.

"How are you, Charles?"

Charles slid his hands into his pockets. "Well—I'm fine. Real fine. Just a little surprised."

"I should have written that I was coming."

"No. Hey. That's all right. It's terrific to see you. I just expected you to be teaching. Did the school burn down?"

"No. I'm on leave. Dean thought I should have a rest. I got a little chaotic after the funeral."

"Is something wrong, Fielding?"

"Wrong? No. Well, I mean I'm not sure."

"Hey, I have some mail for you. I couldn't figure why it was coming to me."

"Letters? There isn't any good news I'm expecting. Did you read them?"

"No. They're yours. I was going to send them to you next time I got to town. Come on. I'll get them."

Charles took his bags, and they moved together up toward the cabins. Behind them lay an ancient, rotting Lincoln Continental with chickens squawking in and out of windows. A roofless outhouse leaned a few yards behind that. Two pregnant women in bright gingham dresses sat talking in a doorway. Chrysanthemum had shed her pajamas and was standing midstream, scrubbed up and down by Ishmael. Children naked or in brief, coarse shirts, darted from door to door. No end to little creatures.

"Are any of those yours, Charles?"

"I don't know. One, maybe. None of us know for sure. A few people have kind of paired up, but most of us move around. This is a commune, Fielding. We do things in different ways."

"I know. I know. Is that one little possibility around someplace?"

"He went to town with Summer and some of the other women."

"A boy?"

"Yeah. Summer's kid."

"Oh."

"What?"

"You know what."

"They're well cared for. I love all of them."

"That kid might be my grandchild. I'd like him over for Sunday dinner someday."

Approaching the cabin farthest from the field. Inside two naked women pulled dough and swiped at flies. A huge pot boiled on a greasy wood stove.

"There's a file cabinet in the kitchen. I put the mail in it. Come on in."

"Should I?"

"Yeah. Of course. They're bare-ass all the time. Nobody cares. Do me a favor, though. Call me Mandrake. We all took different names here. Sort of starting over from scratch. Name and all."

"Name and all. All right."

The two women, both very lumpy, blonde, and tan, smiled and made no attempt to dive for shelter.

"Hey, chicks. I'd like you to meet my father, Fielding Jones. Fielding, this is Aunt Jemima and Persephone."

"How do you do."

"Hey, you're the doctor of philosophy. I dig philosophy. We'll have to talk some time." Persephone's immediate flaw was the absence of front teeth. Aunt Jemima gave him a sweet Sunday morning smile. There were smudges of flour about the hips where she'd wiped her hands. Persephone's breasts were white with it.

"We're flour children," Aunt Jemima said.

"God, you tell that rotten joke fifty times a day."

"Shit, Persephone. That's my business."

"Peace," Charles flashed a sign.

"That's all you ever want, Mandrake."

Charles flushed and turned toward the cabinet.

"Here, Fielding. Telegram care of me and a letter. They both came yesterday. The letter looks like it's from grandma. Let's go outside."

"Come see me some time, professor." Persephone smiled and flung dough to the table.

Charles glared at her. "Okay, Perse. Enough is enough."

"He's a lot bigger than you, Mandrake. You sure he's your father?"

"Come on, Fielding."

Charles led him up a path to a campfire site where deerskins were stretched and drying. Jones sat down on a stump and opened the telegram.

> *Fielding—trustees believed my story. Then Lieutenant Sullivan phoned. Said you were a fugitive. Why? Our time is almost up, my friend. DeJong wants blood. Tomorrow they act. Papers have the story. Will wire results.*
>
> *Dean Vredevelt*

"Jesus."

"What is it, Fielding?"

"Looks like I'm sacked."

"What? You're sacked? That's impossible. They can't sack you. Don't you have tenure?"

"Yes."

"What the hell. You always said they couldn't can you unless you raped a trustee's daughter or got caught pushing dope or something."

"You're close."

184

"What?"

"I was arrested in Des Moines. Possession of narcotics and indecent exposure."

"Don't kid me, Fielding. I don't believe you. You're weird, but you're not perverted."

"Thank you, Charles."

"You're not joking."

"I was cleared of both charges. I thought."

"Hey, you were really busted. That's wild. The cops after you?"

"Apparently."

"My old man gets busted. That's rich. I feel like a goddam father."

"You are."

"Yeah, but this is weird. How'd you get yourself in so much trouble?"

"Long story, Charles. Let me see what mother has to say." He tore the envelope with a trembling thumb.

Son,

I learn of all your badness and my heart is pumping. So sore. Selling to dope fiends is bad, but you also do unspeakable acts to the Brownie Scouts. My life is pain. I bear you like my Saviour's cross. It is all a vale of tears for me. Then old Mr. Velding, your neighbor, called me on the telephone to say you have a naked woman in your house, Miss Horton. Before poor Sarah is in the grave two weeks. I called her on the telephone and read her from the Holy Scriptures. She could say nothing to me, that woman. Now you will kill me with your badness.

Love,
Mother

"You look sick. What is it?"

"There's a bottle in that large case."

"I don't drink anymore."

"I do. More every day."

Charles opened the case and handed over the Canadian. Jones lifting it to his lips, taking a long hot pull. Drown the carking cares. One for poor Miss Horton and her swiftly cooled pants. Our sad harmless desires, smashed with a vengeance worse than God's. Curse the lot of them. You, too, mother. God, what a wretch I am. Deny you motherhood, trusteehood, as you deny me all that I am. Pharisees. Poor Dean. I've ruined you. Ruined us both.

"Go easy, Fielding. That stuff is bad for the body."

"No difference."

"Is grandma all right?"

"Never better."

"I'll take these cases down to my cabin. Can you stay the night?"

"If you'll have me, Charles. I think I'll sit here awhile."

"Be my guest. I've got to get back to the field. We eat at one. Same cabin the kitchen's in."

"I'll pay."

"Hell, Fielding . . ."

Jones drank till one, then dragged himself down to the kitchen where a dozen people and as many children were gathering. The women not pregnant were naked, including Chrysanthemum. They spoke in raucous voices, blurring his mind. Eyes weren't properly focusing. A huge rutabaga steamed in a bowl in the center of the communal table. Aunt Jemima carved hunks and filled children's plates. Bread was cut and passed. And water.

"I'll have a hamburger with everything."

186

Charles smiled and took a seat beside him. "This is my father."

"Welcome." A bald, moustachioed man spoke. He wore gold earrings and a buckskin nightshirt. "We eat only organic foods here. No animal or chemical substances. We are Indian and botanical. It's for purity, you see. We've pledged ourselves to it."

A little boy brushed by Jones and peed out the front door.

"I'm also partial to rutabagas."

"Good. Then let us offer our substance to the House God for blessing."

They raised their plates above their heads, closed their eyes, except Jones. There was much silence, then moustache sang in tremulous voice:

> *House made of dawn light,*
> *House made of evening light,*
> *House made of dark cloud,*
> *House made of he-rain,*
> *House made of dark-mist*
> *House made of pollen.*
> *In beauty it is finished,*
> *In beauty it is finished.*

And all together shouted "Thanks!" and eating commenced with a flash of fingers. Jones, noticing no utensil beside his bowl, scraped up some rutabaga on his fingertips. Charles drank from a jug of clear water and passed it to him. Bread made the rounds and Jones took a quarter loaf. Bland, nauseating rutabaga. Sarah cooked them occasionally. He ate them smothered in steak sauce, but they

187

were still disgusting. To his surprise, the children wolfed them, dipping bread, impaling them on fingers. Charles broke bread and stuffed it in his cheeks. All your etiquette down the drain, Sarah. The trappings of civilization buried with you.

Across the table, a small, dark, pregnant woman watched him. She wore a faded, formless print dress with puffy sleeves. When Jones had finished a half loaf, she spoke.

"Is your name Fielding Jones?"

"It is."

Charles wiped his mouth on his bare arm. "This is Summer, Fielding."

"I have a telegram for you."

"The death knell."

"Something bugging you?"

"Give it to me."

"The pigs are looking for you. Somebody tipped them that you were coming here to see Mandrake. I told them you weren't but they'll probably be out anyway. What do they want you for?"

"Lord."

"They don't seem too uptight about it. Be cool. We can hide you."

Jones's food rushed upward to his throat. "The telegram."

"Yeah. Here it is."

He lurched through the kitchen and out into the afternoon sun. Something dreadful in the air. Hands trembling on the yellow paper. The sun too hot for May. Some disaster due.

He ripped the envelope and pulled out the pasted fragments of a message.

188

Fielding—Everything is finished for us. DeJong has prevailed despite my explanation of fraudulent charges. Marjorie Horton was implicated. I could not deny the evidence. She has left for England. Permanently, I suspect. I'm leaving for Maine within a week. Seeking purer air to breathe.

Ys.
Harold Vredevelt

Down on a stump to consider dappling the sand with long-unused tears. The telegram crumpled in a sweaty fist. Miss Horton. Poor, dear Miss Horton. Wishing only some man to love her before the fires died. Now across the sea and gone, the scabbard forever swordless. I would have come to you again, Marjorie, and played my merry tunes. I see your bottom cold, and lips drawn as time slips out. Lips once a little greasy, moist with warm wine. How many weeks ago? Sitting in your room listening to the radiators pound, Sarah's dress hanging in the closet, as God's good shepherds assailed your already lonely, love-less life. Now cold in the fog of some dank English town. A good woman who waited too long to reveal it, and missed a man. Sad, sad. Praise God for this firm and resolute justice.

He lifted the bottle from a pocket and drained the dregs. Need more to finish this day. Marjorie. Forgive me. I didn't do it, but forgive me. Lily, why did you leave?

"Charles!"

He appeared at the door. "What, Fielding?"

"Come here. I've got to talk."

"What is it? We're meditating . . . join us."

"Come here, dammit. I need you."

He disappeared, then returned with something in his hand. "Okay. We'll go up the hill. More bad news?"

"I guess."

"You look all torn up."

"It's nothing."

"Nothing?"

"Like in Godot."

"You're really canned."

"Worse than that. Slandered. Worse than that. God. Assassinated."

"You?"

"A friend. No one you knew."

"I'm sorry."

"Charles, sit down. Tell me what your plans are. Talk to me."

"Plans for what?"

"For life."

Charles sat in the grass and put a cigarette to his mouth, striking a kitchen match on the heel of his boot. "I'll stay here, Fielding."

"Why? I need a grandson."

"Ha!"

"What do you mean 'Ha!'?"

"Nothing."

"Dammit, Charles, quit being coy."

"You need a grandson. You never needed a son."

"What? Why do you say that? I always wanted you."

"Sure you did."

"Listen, you stuck to Sarah like Elmer's pucky. Wouldn't let me in edgewise."

"You never tried. I can't remember doing anything with you."

"What kind of nonsense is that?"

"Name one time."

190

"I took you fishing."

"You would have gone anyway."

"All right. How about the Big Bear? How about that, Mandrake? Can you deny I played the Big Bear with you?"

"I hated that game."

"Why? Was it too rough?"

"Listen, man, this is a ridiculous scene. All you ever did was sit in a library." He took a deep drag.

Jones blinked. "I was writing my dissertation."

"Wow. Mark Twain's use of Adverbial Clauses."

"That wasn't it."

"Some useless shit like that. Something really worth giving up your family life for."

"So it was useless. It put food on the table."

"So do I. But I take time to love those kids."

"Those kids. I haven't even seen you say hello to one. You don't even know which one is yours. What is that vileness you're smoking?"

"Pot."

"Give me one."

"Here."

"What do I do with it?"

"Inhale and hold."

"I need some Canadian. I'm drunk but not drunk enough."

"That's all I've got."

"Match."

Charles flicked another on his heel and held it near Jones's nose. "Smoking dope with my old man. After all these years something in common."

Jones sucked in a searing lungful. Smoke curling through his teeth. Reclining in a bed of yellow dancing adder's-tongues. Behind Charles, in a birch tree, a huge yellow-eyed owl stared at Jones. Five piercing remarks from the clawed bill, the head swiveling and small, tufted ears leaning windward.

"That beast is looking at me."

Charles turned. "It's Monroe. He's looking for mice."

"He's looking at me. I hope he's a pet."

"There are no pets here. But the animals come and go as they please. We're no threat to them."

Jones scowled, and Monroe, with a crash of wings, took to the sky.

"I don't care for owls."

"How you feeling?"

"Don't know. Too drunk to tell."

"Pot is fine. Finer than that poison you drink."

"That's my business. At least it's legal poison."

"Wow. You talk about legal and every pig from here to Des Moines is looking for you."

"Stop saying *wow*. All you young people ever say is *wow*. Heavy. Pop culture clichés, Charles. I'm disappointed in you."

"I'm used to it."

"What are you trying to prove?"

"Nothing."

"Then come home with me. Bring your paramour and kid, too."

"No way, Fielding."

"Why?"

"I'm learning here. That's why. More than I ever did at the Pines. And when the Big Starve comes I'm going to be ready. All the rest of you meat-eating toilet flushers will die when the supermarkets close. But I'll still be around. And so will my kids, Fielding. But you won't. You won't know how to make it. Look." Charles uprooted a single adder's-tongue and shook the earth from it. "See that bulb? Boil a dozen and you've got a meal. In the summer

192

this place is a blanket of sunflowers. Sixty different kinds. And I know all of them. One kind produces tubers better than potatoes. The seeds are edible. Some you can get oil out of. Man, you gotta be an Indian in this world or you won't make retirement."

"You're a wizard, Mandrake."

"You never take me seriously."

"Come home with me."

"Forget it. What's at home?"

Above them a sky hawk swooped and screamed. Down by the Lincoln chickens squawking, making for the windows.

What's at home? A distressing question. Sundays in the graveyard, placing wreaths.

"Does that Lincoln run?"

"It should. Summer bought a battery today. Why?"

"I want to buy it. Twenty-five bucks."

"Hell, the battery cost fifteen. You don't want it anyway. It's full of chicken shit."

"Forty bucks. No more. I'm leaving."

"Don't. Stay the night. I'm sorry. There's a cave up the hill you can hide in tomorrow. We stash our dope there."

"This whole place is alien to me, Charles. I'm better off somewhere by myself. Too much bare flesh around. All I see is hair and pores. Like Gulliver on that giant tit. But I appreciate the offer."

"Sure."

"I do."

"I didn't expect you to understand this. It doesn't bug me."

"Someday you'll see the mistake. When you're forty-eight dreaming of twenty. When there's no reason to set up a Christmas tree. No one to sit in a boat with."

"You should have thought of that twenty years ago."

"All right, Charles. Go tell the chief about my offer. I'll finish my cigarette and contemplate a course of action."

"Where'll you go with cops looking for you? That chicken coop will never get you home. You'd be better off turning yourself in if you're innocent."

"I will. When I'm ready to. But I've got to think first. By myself. I'll find a woods somewhere."

"Live in the woods?"

"You don't think I can do it, Charles?"

"You're hopelessly urbanized, Fielding. I'd give you a week at the most."

"We'll see."

"Buy an Airstream."

"Your smugness disgusts me."

"I mean it. You have the money."

"You don't know what money I have."

"Well, you ought to have it. You never spent it on mother or me."

"Go talk to your chief mucky muck. I'm wasting time."

"Got her the cheapest casket going, too, Fielding. Right in character to her dying day."

"Vanish."

"I'm not your goddam student."

"Vanish!"

"Nice knowing you."

"You never have, Mandrake."

"Right, man. You hit it just right."

The High Council convened around the shattered remains of the giant rutabaga. The chief curled his drooping moustache, raised his arms, and asked for guidance from House God and Sky God. Summer hauled in the battery and set it on the communal table.

Jones leaned on a cross beam, towering over the group,

194

looming like a thundercloud. Miss Horton in his mind. Her bottom so much finer made than any of these. Ivory-sculpted. Two precise melons. A limited perfection allowed her, soon to be stolen away. Perhaps there'll be a shrine in heaven devoted to it. Charles negotiated in whispers to the dignified gathering. Charles, forever lost to me. I long for a rasher of crackling bacon and a jug of brandy. All this meat about and none to eat. Miss Horton cooked me steak and sausages and little round mushrooms floating in a sauce. Her little mushrooms were very fine, too. Chrysanthemum's are more like beetroot or the bottoms of peaches. No subtlety. Seeing Charles' lips move but not hearing his words. The little boy's face is still visible within the man's. I was always in the library, the adverbial clauses of Mark Twain filling my days and nights. And I know he is right, but can't admit it to him. Tomorrow to the park, Charlie. Daddy's off to his school again. Make pennies. So many hours, days away. A kiss at night after he was asleep. Did he ever know I kissed him? And now I weep. I weep the errors of existence. The home I never made.

And all homes gone now. A house back in Michigan with emptiness and old clothes. Too many reminders of what I've let slip away. David gone first, and with him the hope of a natural child. He frightened me. Backed me off the possible pain of commitment to another. Charles gone because of it, through my fingers for fear. For fear. And Sarah whom I loved but rarely told. And father in the grave gathering fishbait. Mother beyond my reach; from the very beginning of me, beyond my reach. Never a caress that I can recall. An occasional perfunctory kiss and that was it. And what have I done? That mop-headed boy whispering there rarely knew these arms. Nor the kisses while he slept. I kissed you every night, Charles. But I can see you never knew.

195

And what is left? No home here among the savages. Lily lost in the contortions of Chicago. Somewhere in a room with a part of me tucked up inside. But gone and lost, as dead to me as Marjorie. The job I despised but never ceased loving, now lost. Pieces of me scattered about the globe in the heads of students. Not much comfort in that type of immortality. The narrow room in Hackley Hall that I called mine, a home of sorts. Thought they might retire it like a football jersey someday. Where did they put my things? My books. And the dozen years of classbooks, lists of fleeting relationships. I hope DeJong stacked all of it up before the altar and touched a match. And gasped at the smudge and stench.

Every moment of the way, passing from goal to goal, degree to degree, succeeding to the astonishment of all, particularly myself, I could feel failure pressing at the back of my head, spreading its tendrils forward through the floss and whipped cream. B.A., M.A., Ph.D. Bamaphd. Even mother swelling in half-believing pride that little Fielding had turned out. That God had worked a miracle on her errant son and made him well. He'll do the right thing now. The rest can be forgotten. He won't act strange like he used to. Bamaphd has taken care of that.

And there in Charles' face is something of the same. I seek failure in the eyes of others and often find it. My own eyes reflecting in them. I knew I could finally do it, and I have. With the dignity of a dog thumped beneath the tires of a garbage truck. And poor Vredevelt rolling under there with me.

Failure is my whore and lover. I will make my home with her, among the chicken drippings.

"The Council has concluded." Moustache took the battery in his hands and held it aloft. "House God advises that a 1959 Lincoln Continental with new Sears battery is worth sixty dollars. Take it or leave it."

"Highway robbery."

"House God would not be offended with fifty-five dollars, though."

Jones grumbled and reached for his wallet. "House God is a Jew. Fifty-five dollars and you clean out the chicken shit."

"Cool enough. The new brother and sister have their first task."

Honest and Chrysanthemum glanced at each other. Honest frowned, but stood up. "All right, man. I'm getting used to it."

"I been swimming in it today."

Jones dropped the money in the rutabaga bowl, Moustache picking it up and counting.

"Hey, man, this is only fifty-two bucks."

"Discount for paying cash."

"Cough it up or keep the chicken shit."

"Thievery."

"Many thanks. Muchas gracias. Let us smoke the peace weed and celebrate.

> *House made of dawn light,*
> *House made of evening light . . ."*

Out the front door tottered a small boy, tow-headed, thin through the shoulders like Charles. Could he be? Another I won't know. Better not ask. More pain than pleasure finding out. Charles leaving at the back door with Ishmael. No glance in this direction. Silent good-byes once more. Once more my options reduced.

22

On the road again. Some say it's a home in itself, one big concrete mattress. The dark wasn't far away as the sun perched on the Rockies and began to slip down behind. This car big as a small house, snorting occasionally, for the timing's bad and the plugs oily and rusted in. A bit of the grandeur of old remaining: silver buttons to power the windows and much chrome blackened by bird shit. Cushions thick as a fat woman's thighs and cracked leather at the bend of my knees. An aerial that goes up and down, but someone's copped the radio, only a hole remaining. Winding up through foothills and praying for the long life of brakes and transmission. A car's no good unless you pray for it. Give it confidence. Curse it and you'll find a pedal turned to mush beneath your foot. In the back seat there's a cooler of hot dogs, a case of whiskey, and several bags of bread—enough to keep a man for weeks in the mountains. Beside him, a notebook for nature thoughts and philosophical musings. Thoughts of pain and that occasional gasp of joy.

The first of which pierces like an arrow. The feathers in my heart. The child. Was it he? I think it was. Stuck his tongue out at grampa driving away. And grampa knows his own.

The Lincoln curved and climbed through mountains once familiar, once perused by younger, healthier molecules. Boulder had long since disappeared below a shelf of smoke and cloud, and only an occasional cabin intruded on the scene. Red sky at night, a shepherd's delight. Wish I were a shepherd.

He raised the bottle to his lips, then coughed and set it back between the legs to keep it warm. Drumming the wheel with a cold wienie, he sang "Down in Jungle Town" and wondered where he was going.

"Onward and upward!" he urged, and wolfed down the dog. A greyhound roared past, snorting fumes, sending a blast against the side of the Lincoln, which didn't waver.

"There's stability. A granite will. This car won't die without a struggle. Fifty-five dollars was a steal. Ha!"

The sky got darker, the road thinner, and Jones capped the bottle and set it on the floor. Mustn't look over that edge at all. Pray for the well-being of this vehicle. One small failure now and we both take up sky-diving. Drinking keeps the ears from popping, but I best let them pop.

"Dear God, bless these spark plugs, gears, brakes. Amen."

Dark crept up. Jones discovered one dead headlight and another that drifted about up in the trees. Soft bits of rain began to fall and puddles flashed on the concrete slabs. Lights raced down the reflectors on guardrails, red eyes winking evilly. He blinked twice at a dark object in the road, two small steel eyes glowing; the screamless skid of

200

bald tires on puddles, the sickening thump beneath him. Behind now, something dead. And no place to stop. His stomach was suddenly empty, ill, and heart racing.

Interesting the things one leaves in his wake. The windows had fogged up with the force of his breathing; he pushed a chrome button for defrost and moved another to hot air. Nothing happened.

"All right. Save strength for the engine."

Take this dirty handkerchief and wipe my breath. Good to see it verified upon the glass. It's a clear window worries a man.

Up ahead a dirt path pitched off the road. Ease this tank to a crawl. Two tracks that cows might walk and field grass grown high between them. Let's try it, Old Paint, and find a private place to rest till dawn. I'll feed you water from mountain streams and you'll munch the tall grass. Lunge a few hundred yards and I'll let you be. Up! Bottles rattled in the case as they galloped through rocks and ruts a mile. Ahead an opening, a field, a sound of rushing water though there was none to be seen, and Jones turned off the path, coming to rest beneath a walnut tree and shutting off the engine and lights.

He opened a window and a fresh gust of air, delightfully green and wet, struck his fevered brow. The crash of water was loud now, and drowned the quiet splash of rain.

"This must be the place," mumbling and lifting the warm brown bottle for a good-night kiss. Eat a cold dog and sniff the wildness about. It's a bit frightening, but there's something akin to me out there that I'll look for in the morning. Better than a day in Des Moines, at any rate. Move the bottles and cooler to the front and squeeze into this short, soft bed, spreading an overcoat about as much of me as possible. Set one thought to paper on this immense eve:

May 1, 1970

*I hereby transfer all my stock in human existence
to the woodchucks and the peewees.*

Ys.

F. Jones

Morning. The rigid, cramped, frozen body of Jones.
Eyes opening, the mind dragging slowly after. Silk cushions tuck with buttons on the ceiling, like a coffin.

A whirl of rooms and beds in the brain. Where this
morning? Ice on the windows. A steering wheel. I've slept
in a car, it appears. Open the back door and step out to
the crash of cold sun. Mist rising from the valley down the
field from him. He beheld the sight of a lifetime, blasting
his sticky, sleep-filled eyes. Pine trees, oaks, poplars, sumac
fringed two shores of a mountain lake. A creek plunged
down into it, down out of it. There was no sign of human
beings but this road which disappeared in grass a hundred
feet away. Jones pushed the door shut and heard the "ka-
tich" echo through the valley.

"I've stumbled into the garden. Praise the Lord."

His teeth clicking, body quivering, he made his way
down to the shore to find some firewood. There was a jar
of instant coffee in a bag on the floor. Have to boil water
in a hubcap. Little oil never killed a man. A '59 Lincoln
Continental was really all a man needed: a home, a means
of transportation and entertainment and sustenance, a
chicken coop. And only fifty-five dollars, which is a bit
more than what Thoreau paid. But he got less. After breakfast, we'll figure the budget, Henry and I.

Out on the lake a huge fish rolled, startling him. Pink
on the back. A trout, no doubt. No salmon up here. Have
to fashion me a Huck Finn rig and try the luck. Trout for

202

lunch. Inexpressible ecstasy. You've found your calling, Jones. And no one around that you can harm or offend. Water as clear as the air but denser, bluer, rock-bottomed. No Michigan muck-bottom here. Mountains on all sides, locking me in and the world out. New grass racing up the slopes, creeping to the tops, and beyond that, the lonely giants, capped in snow and clouds, taking my breath. What breath there is.

"A fire. Goddammit. This is a miracle. I'll go naked in the afternoon and no one will know. Brownies need not apply."

Loads of twigs and logs lay among the wild violets and umbrella plants. Jones piled them on a flat rock shelf beside the lower creek, a torrent falling six feet then rushing downward, bursting from its bed. Foam and bubbles flew. He pulled dry grass from under the new and stuffed it into the woodpile.

"No matches. I'm doomed."

He rushed to the car, searched the seats, floorboards, glove compartment, but found nothing.

"Cigarette lighter. I'll always be pure, Lord, if it works."

He punched it in and muttered a prayer. In a moment it popped, red and sparking. Rushing to the shelf, he shoved it into the dry grass and blew. The grass smoldered and caught. A twig crackled. Jones saw it was good.

May 2, 1970

Began anew with a breakfast of wieners in pine pitch and oily coffee. Cured a bout of queasiness with a taste of the old gus. Have decided to set down an account of my expenses at the outset of this experiment and to record all other expenses incurred along the way, excluding psychic.

One mobile house	$55.00
Fuel for house	6.77
One case of fuel for owner of house	60.00
Hot dogs	5.65
Bread	.82
Coffee	1.29
Hot mustard	.31
Pepto Bismol	.98
Reading matter (*Sex Pawn*)	.95
Total	$131.77

For this I have gained peace of mind and body, a short bed, a private place to piss, and all in the space of three and one half hours. Cheap enough these days. I'm not lonely or missing anyone. Saw two tortoises mating on a rock. Wanted a closer look, but decided against swimming the rapids. Nature is nice. Kidneys appear to be functioning perfectly. No complaints except that my eyes itch. Believe there's pollen in the air. Nature's intercourse in full blast. Believe I'll read awhile.

F. Jones

A week passed. Jones grew into his bed. No one intruded on his solitude. He sharpened paper clips on a rock, found a long stick and some spring twine from under the front seat and began fishing in earnest. Three days later he caught his first fish, a brook trout with skin cancer. He enshrined it in a fern and set it beneath hot coals, sat down to salivate and fell asleep, discovering the darkened carcass hours later.

May 13, 1970

Man must eat to live, not live to eat. Sex Pawn *is a fine book. Read it for the fifth time this afternoon. Wish I had a boat and a fly rod. Dreamt of Lily again last night. Thoreau must have had the mumps as a teen-ager. Damned pollen is killing me. Keep hoping to find a nymph or a nudist colony in my wanderings. Haven't heard a human voice since I arrived. Only a bus or two grinding gears down the mountain. Talk to myself a lot lately. About Marjorie and Sarah and such. Dream about them, too. Somedays it's difficult to tell dreaming from waking. Yesterday I found red corruption washing down into the lake. Investigate later. Wonder if the cops are giving up? One package of hot dogs left. Have to venture out if the fishing doesn't improve. Tortoises have a hard go of it sexually. Ducks are everywhere. Big flocks of them landing on my lake and moving on. Threw a few rocks but missed. Can't find frogs for frog legs. Think I'll try a hot dog for lunch.*

F. Jones
Naturalist

May 15, 1970

Last dog gone the way of all dogs. Dreamed dead faces floated in my soup, like little oyster crackers. And I ate them. Feel unsteady even though the sun is tanning my arse. Dreams don't leave as easily now. I can walk about half the day entertaining myself with the horrors of the night. Time for introspection in this private place. Too much time. I weep at the drop of a hat.

I wear clothes only when necessary now, when

205

the breeze tightens the scrotum and puts a blossom on the cheeks. I'm eating the bulbs of adder's-tongues. Charles was right about them. They taste like little onions. Got the feeling yesterday that someone was spying. Followed the stream uphill a mile or so and found a stinking sewer pipe which I stopped up with a hubcap. Someone befouling my nest. This evil shall not go unavenged. It argues the depravity of man.

F. Jones
alias, The Green Hornet

The morning of May 20, Jones awoke to the grim glory of his forty-ninth birthday. He munched a Gelusil as he rolled out into the heavy mist, grass cold on his naked feet. Beneath the gray stubble of his beard, psoriasis was making insidious inroads. He felt crawling, dirty. With an overcoat about his shoulders, he walked down to the lake for daily ablutions. At the shore he shrugged off the overcoat; across the lake a small deer herd grazed in the short grass, undisturbed at the strange creature opposite. He found himself gazing sentimentally in the direction of the does. Wonder if Thoreau had any steady animal companions. No mention of them in the journal, though he was a great lover of our furry friends. Man has to love something or other.

Into the freezing water slowly. Let it creep up to the place where it shocks the most. Never was one for pitching in headfirst. Might be an octopus lurking.

The deer suddenly burst for cover. The water touched his left testicle, and he gasped. A gun exploded. Something sliced fifty feet to the left of him.

"Mama mia."

On the shore stood a rawboned old man in bib overalls

206

and a red wool shirt, a shotgun hooked under his arm.

"Hey, you. You're in my lake. Get out or I'll blow you out."

Jones raised his arms. "I surrender."

"Come out of there."

"I'm coming. I have no weapons."

Jones oozed up onto the shore. The old man aimed both barrels at his groin.

"What a sight. A bare-ass hairy old hobo squatting on my land. Get that coat on fast or I'll blast your behind. Ever picked buckshot from your tailbone?"

"No."

"It's a treat."

"I imagine."

"Didn't you see those signs up on the road?"

"What signs?"

"No trespassing. You're a liar if you say you didn't."

"I didn't. My headlights—"

"You're a liar."

"I'm offended at that."

"You hobos and hippies are gonna learn to stay off my land or you'll be more than just offended. I'll drill any hippie comes around here. Some of 'em tried to build a shack here once, but I come in and knocked it down with my tractor. I'll do the same to that junk pile there if you don't move it."

"That fine car?"

"Fine car. Fine for low life like you. I'll be back in here tomorrow morning. If you ain't gone by then I won't miss."

"Have you a deed to this land?"

"You bet I have. It's mine all the way to that upper ridge."

"I'd like to see it."

"You'll see the toe of my boot, hobo. Out by tomorrow or your backside is chopped beef."

"How do I know you own this land?"

The old man grinned and raised the gun. Gums full of jagged stumps and chaw.

"All right. I take your word for it. If it's yours, you ought to know there's a mining company up the ridge pouring poison in your lake."

He shot a wad at Jones's foot. "It don't hurt nothing. They pay me for using my water. None of you bums ever pays a cent. Just piss on my trees and eat my fish. How many fish you catch?"

"One."

"That'll be one dollar."

"Jesus."

"That's cheap."

"Four dollars a pound. My wallet's in the car."

"I'll wait."

Jones trudged up the slope through the tall grass, sneezing as he went—thirteen times in a row between curses. Pollen count was deadly today. This day immemorial. Forty-ninth celebration of that glorious birth. With a gun at my back.

Pick up this wallet and count the remains. Ninety-three dollars and a quarter in the pants. One out of ninety-three is too large a bite. Something basic involved here, a matter of principle. One can be pushed to a wall but not through it.

He returned to the old man, reaching out with a bill. The crooked, freckled hand left the gun for the feel of the crisp green. And suddenly Jones was upon him, overcoat flying, the gun blasting into the tops of trees. Legs flailing crazily, the bare ones his, and the old man responding with shocking strength, pummeling Jones in the rib cage with a fist. Trap this bald face in an armpit and kick the gun away. Lord, the man's a demon.

Spinning down the slope, Jones ripping the head from its socket. Should have observed my long-standing pledge of nonviolence, paid the dollar and suffered only humiliation. They danced to water's edge and fell in. The shock took away the old man's breath and he went limp. Heart pounding, leaning on this nursing home candidate, Jones wondered if he'd committed murder. A little breath. Good. Better than none. Stronger than this leaking bellows in my chest.

The clouds broke and light shone through onto the bald pate still trapped beneath Jones's arm.

"Give up?"

"Nuh."

"You'll be sorry."

"Nuh."

Jones pushed him under and ran like a madman up the bank, through the grass to the gun. He turned to look. The old man teetered in the shallows, wiping out his eyes. Jones walked down with the weapon propped on his shoulder.

"Hurt?"

"No."

"I should shoot you."

"That's my gun."

"But I won't. This is your lucky day. My birthday. You aren't hurt at all?"

"You couldn't hurt nobody."

"Oh yeah?"

"Yeah."

"Well, take that." And with naked Grecian grace, Jones let fly the shotgun, which splashed and sank seventy-five feet out.

"I got another one."

Jones pulled his overcoat shut and buttoned it. "I'll take that one, too."

"You will like hell."

"I have other tricks."

"You'll need 'em."

"Shall we sing?"

"You got one day to clear off my land. I'll bring a cop along tomorrow."

"Tell him to watch his step."

"Hell, you're a mushmelon."

"I use my head."

"I'm a seventy-year-old man."

"You are?"

"Ten years ago I'da tied you in a knot and ate you like a pretzel."

"No one trifles with me."

"Clear out, hobo."

Secure the upper hand, Jones. Scare the liver out of him. Keep him trembling.

Grumbling, shaking out a clogged ear, the old man made his way up the road to a red pickup truck parked behind a boulder. Jones got down on his knees in the grass and began searching for the dollar he'd dropped.

May 20, 1970

Think I've busted a rib on an old man's fist. Spent the day looking at my home of three weeks, since I may be forced to leave it soon, and all my beasty neighbors. Some bittern-like fowl keeps trying to build a nest in the grill of my Continental. I have discouraged her, not knowing whether the duration of our stays would coincide. I have lived on bread and roots for a week and find it not unpleasant,

210

except when breathing on someone, which I rarely do. Have killed nothing but a single sickly fish in my stay, and that I didn't eat. I am a miserable designer of weapons and a worse hunter. When the adder's-tongues are gone I'll either shop the A&P or starve. I'm less an Indian than I suspected. Miss a good porcelain crapper, too, with an Agatha Christie to read.

Creatures come and go fearlessly about me. Can't decide whether it's a compliment or an insult. Wish I knew their names. Some wood ducks live in a logjam downstream from the falls. They're thinking of mating, but I've yet to view the phenomenon. A gray squirrel lives in the bunk above me and sometimes drops objects on my tin roof. The deer come by daily to look and eat. They watch me wash my balls. I've near exhausted my supply of antihistamine, and the fever rages still. Sneezed thirty-three consecutive times this afternoon. The esophagitis has flared up with all these bulbs and tubers. Haven't a single bolus for it, so I may be forced to find a Walgreen's. Give me health and a day . . .

Life in the woods is a superb experience. For alligators. I'm lonely. Sad to admit. Dreaming of ladies I've known with some intimacy. All things of nature are coupled but me. And I haven't many years' coupling left. I am no closer to answers now than when I began. This absurd journey. Vague gropings for things unseen. The Jews looked for signs, and so does Jones. Just one hint that I'm not despicable. Ezekiel trembled nightly under those fierce, ceilinged eyes. My ceiling is higher but the eyes are there burning, hot as suns. Cold as moons.

I've apparently missed a truth along the road. Lost the keys through a hole in my drawers. Lying astride a loving woman has seemed holier, sweeter than any pew, and my finest form of prayer. But what would the domine say to that? Recommend Andrew's Liver Salts for the expulsion of foul thought and vain ambition. Whip the buttocks with a willow switch and give the erection a swift snap as nurses do. Purge daily and avoid rich seafoods, particularly oysters. Then shall you be free to serve.

Chapter nine of Sex Pawn *contains the description of a coital position which astonishes me. It is called "the basket job." I believe I'll break off and study it awhile.*

God bless America.

F. Jones
Semi-naturalist

As the sun set on the first eve of his forty-ninth year and the three-quarter moon appeared, Jones lay in a blanket on the rock shelf, fishing in the pool below the falls. Creeping to him, the notes of strange birds and the gloomy aria of owls. And on the water, below the boiling release of energy, the frantic movement of little fish, shocking the pond's surface. The sky was full of stars and moons and planets in hunter's shapes and dogs and dippers. There were little tugs at the line but nothing very bold. And thoughts wandering in the heavens, the eternity of sky. How lost and small I am down here on my rock. How good it would be to have some other with me. A woman or child. A tickle of grief darting like a tongue in the heart. The trees loom like ghosts, moonlight flashing in their eyes. Or are they the underbellies of leaves? Jones, you're going

212

daft. Feeling very queer and sad, like giving it all up. Ceasing to resist. For what's ahead at forty-nine?

So very harmless. Old Jones. Time to start the Geratol. Pep the pizzle with a surge of iron.

Up the road the sound of tires churning and the red pulse of flashers spilling blood in the trees. Jones rolled over and froze. A red pickup truck slid to a dusty stop beside the Lincoln. Then a Colorado State Police car. And another pickup truck.

Jones wrapped the blanket about him and dashed for a clump of cedars. Above the roar of water, the voices trailed faintly down to him.

"Those are the same as this hubcap, officer. He's the one who done it."

"Don't look like the hobo's around. I give him a beating this morning, so he probably lit out when he saw me coming back."

"I'll report in and we'll have a look."

"Don't worry about him jumping you. He's weak as tea. Runs around stark naked most of the time."

"How do you know, Herb?"

"I been watching him from the ridge a couple days now."

"You see him cover the pipe?"

"Naw. But I know he done it."

"Okay."

Twigs snapped and he watched the three of them switch on flashlights and spread out over the field. Jones leaned steathily around a trunk, holding the blanket tight with one hand. Should have taken to wearing clothes after the trauma of the morning. He lifted a stone and tossed it high. It hit the ledge and caromed into the water. Lights flashed toward it and, blanket flying, Jones ran between trees and leaped a barberry bush. Slight miscalculation covered the arse with scrollwork and ripped off the blanket. He fell forward on his knees, biting back blasphemies, and crawled swiftly through the grass.

"He's by the falls! Heard him jump in over by that ledge. Come on, officer. We'll catch your crook."

Old Injun trick never failed. Why are the things I do for right always wrong? Thought I'd be praised for plugging that pipe. Whoa. Two little eyes staring me down, right in my path to freedom.

"Dissolve, beast."

The eyes blinked and disappeared in a scramble. There's respect. Up now on two legs. Pray there's no one waiting in the trucks. Knees bleeding and lungs up in my mouth. Lights now sweeping the empty water. Ease the door open and slide in. Jesus, I'm blocked on three sides. Have to swing into the field to get by. Turn this key with great delicacy. A positive response. God bless Sears Roebuck.

"He's in the car! Quick! He'll get away!"

"We got him blocked!"

No one blocks the way of Jones. On with the light and into gear, ripping up yards of sod and roaring into the field directly at three terrified figures diving for cover. Whip this wheel hard and we'll be on the road again. Should have pulled their plugs before I left. What was that ghastly sound? Praise the Lord, the steering's gone. My car's had a stroke. Hit the brakes, but the lake has sneaked up faster than expected. All is lost. Ego baptizo te in nomine patris. Over the ledge and away.

Jones sat with the windows up as the officer struggled to open the door. With a large sigh, he felt the water reach his neck. The door opened. He didn't move. Hands fastened roughly to him. They floated him out.

"Save the whiskey," he sputtered.

"Gotcha!" they cried.

214

23

Jones sat in his private cell, safe at last. Thirty days' free lodging was preferable to five hundred dollars, particularly for someone with nowhere to go. There was a shave and haircut thrown in besides. And a stool in the corner to while away the hours on. No more backing into trees.

A scalped, sheepish young man sat in the next cell, biting his calluses. "What you in for, man?"

Jones seated himself on the canvas bunk. "Existing."

"I dig. But what are you in for?"

"Vandalism, trespassing, resisting arrest."

"Hey, not bad. I'm here for burning draft files. Ten days and I'll be out doing it again. How long they got you for?"

"Thirty days."

"Yeah."

Won't mention the charge pending in Des Moines. Don't wish to disillusion youth. Smell of vomit in the air. Makes the food taste sweet. Think I'll close my eyes and sleep away all thirty. Dream of better days and beds.

215

"What's the food like, young man?"

"Shit. Mush for breakfast, mush for lunch, hot dogs for dinner. Pure shit."

"Thank you."

On the train to Des Moines, Jones watched his reflection in the glass. There was more gray now that new hair had sprouted. Old on all the edges and tired inside. Content to stare at the little Nebraska towns huddled on the plains and to absorb the warmth of this first summer day. But dimly curious as to what anonymous benefactor had spared him the final week of incarceration. It was Vredevelt, no doubt, the only ally through all this loss. Dear Dean, I tip my wig to your beneficence.

They stopped in Bird City to drop a passenger. The fume-faced hulk of an officer beside him stood up.

"Want to use the toilet, Jones?"

"No thank you."

"Well, I got to. Don't pull nothing while I'm gone."

"I won't."

The officer left, and Jones glanced down the aisle at the open door. Outside, the dark corners of Bird City promised shelter and freedom. But he didn't move. In a few minutes the officer returned and flopped down beside him.

"Good boy."

"I am."

"I can always trust the perverts. They're always too chicken-shit to run."

Jones cleared his throat and closed his eyes.

"I mean, you guys that whip it out for little girls are really afraid of what a woman might do. You're scared of anything with tits. And a real man terrifies the shit out of you. Right? You have to get your jollies somewhere, so you

216

pick on harmless kids. I been to school. I know this crap. Aren't I right?"

Jones said nothing.

"Yeah, I am. You know I am. You don't have to answer. I know what you're thinking. I've known tons of you guys. You make yourselves sick, don't you. You make me sick."

Watching out the window at the blur of poles. How simple to unseat one's faith in the absolute existence of things. Those poles are speeding by, the earth with them too, and I am fixed, a point of stasis, upon which the world plays its ghastly joke. When all alternatives fail, man can, as a final, futile gesture, cease acting and suffer the dole prepared him. Another Jones would have dashed the smugness out of this warden of righteousness. No more. All that absurd rebellion was the struggle of a slave who believed himself free. The new Jones, born full-blown on the half shell, awaits the platter.

In Des Moines he was greeted briefly by Lieutenant Sullivan, then led to jail to spend three days in the tank with four sick winos and a Mexican phrenologist who squeezed his scalp and explained his brains were knotted in turmoil and bad times could be expected. Perhaps even a period in jail. He suggested Jones eat wheat germ and strawberry yogurt to counterbalance strongly negative impulses emanating from the frontal lobes. But Jones secretly knew the answer was lobotomy.

His case came up; he was offered counsel but refused. In the steaming, noisy courtroom, he waited through two child beaters and one sex fiend before he was allowed the witness stand. A damp, bovine clerk confronted him, told him to stand and raise his hand.

"State your full name."

217

"Fielding S. Jones."

"What does the S stand for?"

"Sunshine."

A bit of a ripple around the room.

"Do you swear to tell the truth, the whole truth, and nothing but the truth, so help you God?"

"What is truth?"

The grim, orbicular judge shook a jowl and plowed out his throat. "Please discontinue the metaphysics, Mr. Jones. Answer the question."

"I do."

"We're pleased you do." Another flutter from out front. The judge pursed his lips, trying not to appear delighted.

The clerk tucked in his teeth and sat down.

Again the judge: "Mr. Jones, you are charged with indecent exposure and unlawful flight to avoid prosecution. How do you plead?"

"I plead not guilty."

"And you have refused legal counsel?"

"I have."

"Proceed with your questions, Mr. VanDellen."

A Dutchman for a prosecutor. Perhaps some vague sympathies might generate through the ozone. Probably a Catholic, though. VanDellen approached, looking oily, his baggy blue suit carrying evidence of many luncheons.

"Mr. Jones, where were you at approximately two thirty on the afternoon of April 27?"

"I was urinating in the woods."

A whoop rose from the stands.

"Order! Any more of this childish snickering and I'll clear the room. Proceed, Mr. VanDellen."

"Was the woods you speak of Potter Park woods, Mr. Jones?"

"I suppose it was."

218

"You suppose it was? Weren't you sure? Had you been drinking?"

"One must drink before he urinates."

VanDellen smiled grimly. "Mr. Jones, why weren't you sure you were in Potter Park?"

"I'd never been in Des Moines before. It was a park six blocks from the Rudolph Hotel."

"I see. Would you tell the court what happened in Potter Park woods that day?"

"I was suffering from a kidney infection that had weakened my powers of retention. I was in the park when the need arose. There wasn't an available bathroom, so I had no choice. I went into the woods and a troop of Brownies happened upon me."

"Girl Guides, Mr. Jones. It's an organization for disadvantaged urban children, the purpose of which is to reveal nature's secrets for their benefit."

"Yes."

Again, an uproar and the furious hammering of the judge.

VanDellen cleared his throat and continued, unruffled. "Was that all there was to the experience, Mr. Jones? Did anything else occur?"

"Yes."

"Well?"

"Before I could get my trousers up, a woman, the troop leader, attacked me."

VanDellen bit back a smile and glanced at the judge. Jones, shifting in his seat, wished to be safe in a cell again. Focusing upon the room, he became aware of a malign presence in the front row. That glowing evil eye upon him. Grinelda herself.

"What do you mean she attacked you?"

"She came at me."

219

"For what reason?"

"I wasn't sure."

Swift glance at Grinelda to see that eye filling with blood. About her, a wave of half-suppressed tittering.

"And then what happened?"

"I dodged her and she fell into a huckleberry bush."

At the back of the court some satanic figure applauded. A few others joined. The judge attacked his desk with the gavel.

"Order! This courtroom will not be turned into a Roman circus. If you insist on making light of a most serious situation, I'll clear you out and proceed privately."

Pray they continue. There's been enough public humiliation today.

"Thank you, your honor. I have only one other question for Mr. Jones. It is difficult to present it without seeming very blunt—"

"Ask it, Mr. VanDellen. The courtroom is no place for mincing words."

"Yes. Quite right. Mr. Jones, you said these Girl Guides came upon you while your trousers were down."

"Yes."

"Why were your trousers down?"

Nothing a man can keep to himself. All secrets at last exposed.

"I object."

The judge leaned out over his desk. "On what grounds, Mr. Jones?"

"He's poisoning the wells."

"You should have accepted counsel, Mr. Jones. Objection overruled. Answer the question."

"I've forgotten it."

VanDellen hunched over the rail, a foot from Jones's face. The scent of garlic and sausages nearly overwhelmed him. "Why, Mr. Jones, were your trousers down? If you were urinating in the woods, why were your trousers down?"

"Well . . ." Staring full at Grinelda, whose eyes slipped to the floor, rejecting such body talk. "You've never had an infection of the kidney?"

"No, I haven't."

"Judge?"

"Uh, why yes. As a matter of fact . . . Mr. VanDellen, approach the bench."

VanDellen leaned over the desk, the judge wincing slightly. There were a few whispered words, VanDellen nodding profusely, the judge bending sideways to escape the swamp of garlic.

VanDellen straightened. "I withdraw that last question, your honor. No further questions."

Thank God for the universality of imperfect kidneys.

"Do you wish to cross-examine yourself, Mr. Jones?"

"No, your honor."

"Very well. Call your next witness, Mr. VanDellen."

VanDellen smiled nervously and nodded to Grinelda. "I wish to call Miss Grinelda Wolpot to the stand."

Without a moment's hesitation, Grinelda charged forward. She scowled at the clerk as he swore her in. VanDellen warily approached her.

"Miss Wolpot, I'll try to make this as quick and painless as possible."

"I certainly hope so."

"Do you find any discrepancies in Mr. Jones's version of the story?"

"Of course."

"Would you explain?"

"Mr. Jones says he was relieving himself. I say he was laying for us. Just waiting there to show his . . . his . . ."

"Yes, Miss Wolpot?"

"His nasty thing to my poor little girls."

"I object!"

"On what grounds, Mr. Jones?"

"It's not nasty."

Suppressed hilarity from the groundlings. More frantic rappings of the gavel.

"She's begging the question!"

"Objection sustained. Strike the word 'nasty' from the record."

Grinelda burning holes through my forehead. All that fire could be entertaining, rightly used.

"Miss Wolpot, I want you to think carefully. When you came upon Mr. Jones, what was the expression on his face?"

"I didn't notice his face."

With a snort, the judge swiveled away, lips squeezed up in his hand. "Forgive me," he cried. "Oh, dear, I've never done this before. Order!"

VanDellen bent his head and bit his lip. Grinelda looked actively volcanic.

"Clerk! Get me some water. Hehehe. Oh, dear. Continue, Mr. VanDellen," wiping out his eyes with a huge hankie.

"Uh. Yes. Yes. Miss Wolpot . . . what was I saying? Er—was there no noticeable emotion on Mr. Jones's face when you came upon him?"

"What?"

"Was Mr. Jones surprised?"

"Of course he was."

VanDellen paused for breath. "Are you sure, Miss Wolpot. You understand what your answer means, don't you?"

Grinelda's jaw trembled, cracked slightly. A deep puce

crept from under her lace dickey. "I mean, he was faking it, of course."

"I see. Did you attack him?"

"I—I ran at him to hold him until the police arrived. He tripped me and I fell into a bush."

"Thank you, Miss Wolpot. No further questions, your honor."

"Do you wish to cross-examine, Mr. Jones?"

"I wish to call another witness first."

"Very well. Step down, Miss Wolpot. My apologies."

Grinelda slunk by him and dropped into her seat. There was a time when such revenge might have been savory. Now it's only self-preservation. Just want to get old without interference, Miss Wolpot.

"Well, Mr. Jones?"

"Lieutenant Sullivan of the Des Moines Police Department."

The brave Lieutenant approached, and with bifocals down the nose, read Miss Wolpot's letter. Grinelda returned to the hot seat. Jones leaned up next to her face, trading stares. First to blink was she.

"Does he have to stand so close?"

The judge glanced at VanDellen, who shrugged. "Mr. Jones?"

"Excuse me, Miss Wolpot. I'll stand my distance. Is it my breath?"

"It's you."

"Well, four simple questions. That's all I'll ask of you. Tell me, did you write the letter the Lieutenant just read us."

"Of course I did."

"Stating that if I apologized publicly to the Grand Exalted Council of the Girl Guides, the charge against me would be dropped?"

"You know I did."

Noticing for the first time, Grinelda, what large chests you have.

"Did I attend your meeting of the Grand Exalted Council?"

"You did, but—"

"And did I say, before all the ladies of your organization, that I was sorry about the embarrassment caused you?"

"No!"

A little lady leaping up in the front row. "He did, Grinelda. Tell the truth."

"Shut up, mother!"

"Order! Order in this court! Miss Wolpot, did Mr. Jones tell you he was sorry?"

A long pause as Grinelda's eyeballs began to twitch. "Well . . . yes. But—"

"But what?"

"But it was the way that he said it—"

"He did say it then?"

"Yes. But wait—"

"And Mr. Jones, did you leave Des Moines under the impression that the charge had been dropped?"

"That's right, your honor."

"Mr. Jones, Mr. VanDellen. Approach the bench."

"Wait! I have more to say—"

"Enough, Miss Wolpot. Quite enough. I'd suggest that you reread the Golden Code of the Girl Guides of Des Moines, which I, by the way, helped draft. About keeping your word through thick and thin, straight and narrow, something like that."

"Well!"

"And though I don't condone relieving oneself in a public place, I do think you should learn the difference between an honest urination and an indecent exposure."

224

Furious applause from out front. The judge acknowledging with a nod.

"And you, Mr. Jones, should learn better manners. You are an educated man. I should expect that you'd know enough to stay close to home when your kidneys are inflamed. I, myself, do not leave the house at all. You should also perceive that such outdoor activities are ecologically unsound. I've written a pamphlet on human waste and our environment. I'll require you to buy a copy. One dollar. Case dismissed. Court adjourned until three."

A cheer rose from all the unknown friends and well-wishers. Grinelda got up slowly, creakily, aided by mother, struggled across the floor, eyes as close to teary as they'd probably ever been. Taking something from a purse as she passed, she gave it a nasty flip against my guts. A letter.

"There, you beast."

"What is it?"

"Read it. I hope it gives you an ulcer."

"Thank you."

Mother hauling her down the aisle and out of my life. You're one I won't miss. Poor lady. One swift plow might have made the difference. All that idle flesh. Make a good climb for an Eagle Scout. A new merit badge for mound bounding.

Open this strange missive with trepidation. A Michigan address on the envelope: 1251 Shrewsbury Drive, Bloomfield Hills. Whom do I know in the high society of Detroit? No one, I think. I'll read and see.

June 10, 1970

Dear Miss Wolpot:

Your answer to my letter was most disconcerting. I know Mr. Jones is not guilty of these allegations

225

because I was in his company immediately before
and after your encounter with him . . .

Trembling in the hand. These broad, flowing letters have a familiar ring.

> *. . . He is not the kind of person you say he is.*
> *Please drop the charges you have made. I am* beg-
> ging *you. Otherwise I shall be forced to testify in*
> *his behalf. That would be embarrassing for both of*
> *us.*
>
> *There is a further reason I ask this of you. It is*
> *difficult to reveal, but you have compelled me to.*
> *I am carrying Mr. Jones's child. I do not want him*
> *to know it. He may feel an unnecessary responsibil-*
> *ity to marry me. This problem I consider more my*
> *doing than his. One error has been made. I don't*
> *want to make another. If I am forced to take the*
> *witness stand, he will know everything.*
>
> *I have already lost a job through this indiscre-*
> *tion. I do not wish to lose anything more.*
>
> *Once again, I* beg *you to drop all charges.*
>
> *Very sincerely,*
> *Lily Robertson*

Slumping into a chair, the noise abruptly subsiding with the echoed boom of a door, he watched three fat pigeons tryst on a windowsill, the sun pouring through. Dusty ghosts floated in the beams. God momentarily staggering in his heaven. Jones sustaining serious emotional disorientation, agony and ecstasy, absurdity and sublimity. A child from these unflagging, ageless loins. There's birth control, Lily. What a blow you must have dealt them at the clinic.

226

And a sudden stroke of fear for the monster possibly produced. An epileptic mongoloid. My God. Another David would be the end of me. Even with Lily there to share the grief. Or joy. Why didn't she come, I wonder? Fatherhood at forty-nine, Lord, I can't believe it. This morning I'd have been delighted to muddle into senility and grampahood. Now this. I loved you back there, Lily. I think. Mustn't think. Thinking is a curse. A crime. I'm coming, Lil, to claim the little bugger, whatever he is. And you. Half alive again with thoughts of you.

And Jones standing up, erect, proud, raising his chin in triumph.

"Yahoo, wow!" he said.

And no more needed saying.

24

In the dazzling chrome can of a Whisper Jet, Jones strove to scrape off the prison pallor and reconstruct the Original Man. Scratch these scummy teeth with a thumbnail. Hair half-grown, crazy; need an iron to press it down. And all that gray so sudden it's frightening. Grizzling every day in my cell, while I considered the qualities of emptiness. Forget the face. Nothing to be done now. She's the kind who'll take me as I am, for better or worse. Dear Lily. In your belly lives the key to the kingdom, the peace denied me. A simple thrust of the loins and eureka. Sarah and I thrusting twenty years with indiscernible results. Thrice a week. Three thousand one hundred and twenty times, to be exact. And nothing to show but worn parts and David.

Plunging into Detroit Metro at nine in the morning, the sky afire with violent sun. Heat mists rose already from the runways as the day edged up on July. I'll marry her Independence Day with a volley of Roman candles. If she's returned to father, as I figure, I may stand to gain a few cents in the bargain. Sixty-three dollars for a sky ride and breakfast pains the soul, but there'll be compensations. That long body, mine day and night. Provided I can manage. Change it to weekly in a few years, if she doesn't object.

Through the heavy sun in a shuttlebus, Jones lamented the ten dollars to Bloomfield Hills. A load of summer theater goers bound for The Horse's Mouth babbled about the obscurity of T. S. Eliot's plays, touching a sentimental chord. Wonder if DeJong has finished me for good. I should have taken the bastard to task. To court. Beat the holiness out of him. Feeling ornery as hell again, a healthy sign.

"Excuse me." A plump, profoundly rouged woman touched his arm. "Do you mind if I smoke?"

"I beg your pardon?"

"Do you mind if I smoke?"

"I'm being married the Fourth of July."

"Wonderful. Do you mind if I smoke?"

"Yes."

Up Terwilliger Street to Shrewsbury. All this stone and marble makes the guts quiver and yearn for a Gelusil. Haven't had a tonic or pill for a month. One doesn't need vitality in a cage. Now that I'm living again, it's my duty to sustain strength. Perhaps I'll be a tonic tester for my new papa-in-law. Specialize in love potions and kidney energizers.

The bus slid to a halt in front of a high-brick wall with an open iron gate. 1251 in metal script at the top of the

230

bricks. Jones thanked the driver, got out, and stood at the gate in a fog of diesel fumes. The bus disappeared around a corner.

I've seen this all somewhere before. In a dream. In *Gone With the Wind.* A colonnade of willows all the way to the house. A monstrous brick bastion with parapets and battlements and towers, worthy of Al Capone. But somehow warm under all the willows, because Lily is there. That Christian dungeon in Des Moines looked pleasant with her in it.

God, I'm trembling like a pimply boy come a-courting. Do I ask the old man for her hand while she sits in the parlor feeling little Fielding kick? Act now, think later, my motto all these years.

He walked the long asphalt driveway to the door, touched a button and activated Handel's *Messiah* on the bells within.

An aged black man opened to him.

"Could I help you?"

"Have the wrong house."

"This is the Robertson residence."

"You're not Mr. Robertson."

"Certainly not. I'm the butler."

"Oh. My God. Well. I'm looking for Miss Lily Robertson. Is she home?"

"No, she isn't."

"Do you expect her?"

"No."

"I've come a long way. I'm an old friend. Where is she?"

"I'm not free to tell you."

"Not free to tell me! Listen here, I'm going to marry her."

The cracks around his eyes abruptly increased; he seemed near to toppling over. "Oh my."

"You've got to tell me where she is."

"Oh, my my."

Jones grasped the tiny shoulders and shook. "Where!"

"Haven't you heard, sir?"

"Heard. Heard what?"

"She was married yesterday."

Jones staggered back, dragging the old man along. A willow branch swept the back of the neck like a woman's fingers.

"Let me go, sir."

Dropping his arms, leaden weights, leaning back on the railing. "My God. Who'd she marry?"

"Mr. Bradley, sir. One of Mr. Robertson's vice-presidents."

"But that's my kid she's carrying."

"I thought as much, sir."

"Where are they?"

"At his apartment. But they're leaving today for the Virgin Islands."

"The address."

"In Detroit. Downtown. 18 Sweetland Boulevard."

"Good-bye."

"Good-bye, sir."

Out into the road for a taxi but none to be found. Damnable things always conspiring against me. Gulf station down the road. Run to it and phone one up. Blot all thoughts from the mind but annulment and murder. There must be some law about eminent domain or original entry. Lily, if I've lost you, both of you, I'm buried. One of the old man's vice-presidents. You sold out so completely, when a nice older fellow would have gladly squatted beside you at the altar. If you'd only known how innocent I was. Am. Lily.

Forty-five minutes and he was downtown, sweating out the pinwheeling meter. Six more bucks and I'm destitute. Sweetland Boulevard on the sign. Sixteen bucks for a bloody ride. That's enough for a decent car of my own. Rows of rundown brownstones and lots of black faces. Doesn't look like vice-president territory. Up ahead a thirty-story cement and tinted glass building.

"That it?"

"That's it, bud."

They stopped, and with a nasty look Jones handed over the money and dashed inside. Fountains splashed and gurgled, exotic birds warbling in huge cages. The air-conditioning hummed at full steam. People milled about in the lobby, some watching a Tiger game on a large color set mounted above the desk. A kid sailed an aircraft carrier in the fountain, shooting birds from the deck.

"Dow! Dow! Dow! Dow!"

Jones went to the desk, arousing a huge, pea-headed woman from the ball game.

"Those clowns can't win without McLain."

"Mr. Bradley's room, please."

"Mr. Bradley is just leaving for his honeymoon. Out there in the parking lot. See?"

Through a wall of plate glass, Jones saw Lily's orange dress, the auburn hair flung back, Bradley leaning into the trunk of a Cadillac.

"Don't you play any tricks on them. Last night someone filled their bed with rice. Say now, you'll get the sunstroke."

Out the door and into the pounding heat. Over a row of parched hedges and onto concrete.

"Hey!"

Lily turned; small beads of sweat glistened on her temples. Her belly was hidden in the loose folds of the dress.

"Lil!"

Bradley looked up from the trunk, smiling, sweeping blond locks from his forehead. Young and smooth and good-looking. With a purple Cadillac.

Jones slowed to a trot, approaching her.

"Fielding." Tears welled in her green eyes. Centuries since I've looked into them.

"Lil . . . all those charges . . . I was innocent."

"Why did you come?"

"I read Miss Wolpot's letter."

"Oh."

"I believe I love you."

Tears popped out and rushed down her cheeks in dark streams of mascara.

"Please go away."

Bradley straightened up, buttoning his jacket. "Hey, what is this?"

"That's my baby, Lil. Not his. Why didn't you let me know? Dammit, I had a right."

"Go, Fielding. I'm already married."

Bradley approached him. "So this is the bastard."

"Vanish, child-stealer."

A fist circling under his nose.

"Don't touch him, Arnold."

"Lil, please. I love you. I want the kid. Annul it. Plead temporary insanity. I'm begging."

But her eyes disappeared as she slumped backward into the open rear door of the Cadillac, grabbing it shut after her.

"Lil! I won't have you marrying that curd face! I'll fight for you!"

Bradley, who had turned a shade of beetroot, was upon him, threatening cops and murder, tearing at his collar, slamming him backward into a hedge. Jones watched a fist

234

launch itself into the middle of his face. Seeing the hedge, the sky in flashes. Slipping through the greenery onto an alleyway. Cement hot on the back, sun searing the brains, Jones rose to see Bradley disappear into a phone booth at the front of the building. He blew blood and pushed back through the hedge, hearing Lil's sorrow in the back seat, seeing her face buried to the ears in a lap robe. Dear God, Lily, you are a weeper. Wish you'd quit a moment. There are several things we should discuss without hubby listening.

Jones bent in grinning but she wouldn't look. Keys in the ignition. There's a temptation. Bradley's distracted, bellowing something in the receiver, and I've never driven such a noble beast before. I'll borrow both of you a while. Quietly now with this key. And how softly it purrs to life. I'll sneak like a sheik.

Swing low, purple Cadillac,
Coming for to carry me home . . .

Almost out the driveway before Bradley turns and screams, ripping at the phone booth door which refuses to fold. Bloody traffic nose to nose for miles, so I must rudely make a place and offer apologies. Sorry, madam. No need to display such villainous looks. Many more feel as you do. Bradley, for instance, who is suddenly alongside, running as if bulls were behind him, trying to open the door opposite me. God's bones, the man's a maniac. Slight swerve to the right pancakes him against a mailbox. I glance back with trepidation to see him rise up howling, with no apparent damage. There's true resilience; the man has solid flesh and a hint of spirit. Hasn't occurred to me that she might be in love. Perhaps when she looks up

235

I'll find her hating me. There's a thought that wilts the heart.

Jones drove silently down the boulevard into the ferocious eye of sun. A river smell drifted in at the windows; he glanced at Lily, who was quieter now, and fought the first tendrils of despair.

Thinking, Sarah. How are you, love? I need some order about me now.

He pulled his sleeve across his mouth and came up covered with blood. Then, a broken, faraway voice, "Forgive me. I'm sorry for this. I'll make it up to you, Arnold. Life is hell for me sometimes."

"But worth the price, all things considered."

Abruptly she was upright and bristling. "Where's Arnold! What are you doing here? This is his car."

"I only wanted to talk, Lil. Arnold had to mail a letter."

"Mail a letter? What are you saying? Where is Arnold? Oh, I don't believe it. This is a nightmare." She put her knuckle in her mouth and bit down hard, tears pouring out over her hand.

"Lil. Good gravy. Oh man. Listen, tell me something now and spare me grief. Do you love that young fellow?"

But she couldn't answer through the flood. A real tidal wave. I never saw so much water out of two eyes. Maybe it's what keeps them green.

"Am I a fool, Lil? Tell me I am and I'll go away for good."

A moment, and the sobbing slowed.

"I'm married. Don't you understand?"

"Nobody's perfect."

"Arnold is my husband."

"But am I a fool?"

A long, deafening silence.

"Yes. Yes."

Shock waves surged up the vertebrae like mallets on a

236

marimba. Slowing this long, cool, purple car to a halt in midstream of a traffic lane, amid a blare and railing from fellow travelers, Jones opened the door and leaned out. But a hand clamped his neck, a grip of steel.

"Drive me, Fielding."

"Lil?"

"Just drive me."

Wordlessly, fearing to unbalance what was in the air, Jones aimed into an express lane and slid through afternoon haze toward a route out of the U.S.A. To his shock a sign instantly appeared, pointing the way, and, after a moment, stark against the sky, the dark webwork of the bridge.

"Fielding. I don't know what I'm doing. It's too late."

Jones pounded the wheel with a fist. "Dammit, Lil, you never gave me a chance. I deserve to be a part of this. I don't just pull out of things when the going gets tough."

"I didn't want you marrying me out of a misguided sense of duty."

"So you rushed home and grabbed the first vice-president handy."

"It wasn't that way, Fielding."

"Did you really believe I was a criminal?"

"No. I mean I learned that you weren't. I wrote your son."

"You wrote Charles?"

"He was very helpful. He let me know of your whereabouts whenever he knew. But he lost track of you after the jail in Boulder. In his last letter he said he had raised some money to bail you out. He was proud of you, Fielding. Few men will risk their own well-being to save the environment. I was proud of you, too."

And in an instant she was over the back of the seat and pressing against my bloody shirt. But I'm swallowing too

237

many sentimental lumps to respond. All this news is too much like fantasies I'd filed away forever. Charles Jones acknowledging his birthright and bailing out old dad. So many sensations at once, it's hard to erect the proper restraints.

"Fielding, are you all right?"

"Grand, Lil," biting the lip to check a weak dripping about the nose and eyes.

"What did I say?"

I'd best try something physical or turn to mush before her eyes. Get this long arm around her back and startle the base of one breast with a thumb.

"Fielding!"

It's clear I've forgotten the power of this maiden. With a mighty jerk, she pulls away and heaves me half across the car. A row of garbage cans falls like dominoes before my charging purple chariot.

"Lil, that move was ecologically unsound."

"I almost killed us."

"What's that noise?"

"I believe there's a garbage can caught underneath."

Behind I see sparks tumble out like jacks on the cement, reminding me of an earlier scene I'd prefer not to repeat. They'd give me twenty years for cremating a Cadillac. More for stealing the owner's wife. Some blocks away a siren begins to wail, and acute paranoia attacks all vital organs.

"Take a walk with me, Lily. This car requires too much concentration. There's the bridge. We'll hike over it and figure out a plan."

Grinding into a tow-away zone, Jones tossed open the door and rolled out.

"It's no use, Fielding."

"Hell, Lil, nothing is irrevocable. Charles has proven

238

that. I want you. You know I do. I'll sue Bradley. I'll fight a duel. Come on now."

Though she seemed reluctant, Jones yanked her out into the sun and sweat. A little scream and she was pacing beside him, out the alley and up through a narrow street of paralytic houses and baking bodies immobile in doorways, watching. A long block of stores burnt out and windows boarded, then the smell of river and busy streets. Lungs feel as though someone's building fires in there.

"I'll slow down and let you catch your breath, Lil."

"I'm not out of breath, Fielding."

"Oh."

"I'm mad to be doing this."

"But something makes you do it."

"I should go back."

"Hold my hand and keep walking. We'll get way up in the breeze on that bridge. The air will clear your head."

And before she can answer we're off again, jogging through traffic, hedges, parking lots, by a duty-free liquor store which awakens desires and appetites long suppressed. My kingdom for one long pull of smooth Canadian grain. Read once that such craving was the mark of incipient alcoholism, but know it's another Calvinistic ruse to trick us out of pleasure. Got to watch those folks or they'll rule the world.

"Hold me close for a moment, Lil."

Eating pie, a blueberry hanging in the cleft of his chin, the gourd-bellied officer leaned out the door of his little house, smiled, and waved them on. "Just watch out for the scaffolds. There's a crew painting today."

"Thank you. Sally and me are just married."

Keep her clasped tight beside, hips together like two steers butting in a field, and I gaze down over her, lingering there as I have been unable to do since this absurd frolic began. Lily, your face is soft and open as a flower, guileless and clean and dear to me. Now that I look I think I'm not wrong in this madness. Lily. Lily. Name feels sweet on my lips. Young breasts make me suddenly want to make joyful sounds, eyes tumbling over them, a pounding inside that isn't lust but something forgotten years and years. I'm all alive to you, Lily. Feel me. I want to touch my son and let him know I'm here.

"Fielding! Please."

"I want to feel him, Lil. Just a moment."

And she allows it.

"He isn't moving yet. It's too early."

"He's there, though."

"Yes.

"The doctor says maybe two."

"Two!" Jones leaping at a girder and swinging round it. "Two!"

Lily with her first fine smile in ages. "I don't know. That's what he says."

"Oh brother! Hahaha! Oh, by Jesus, look at that."

"What?"

At the base of the bridge two wolves howled with red eyes flashing. They opened their steel jaws and small men tumbled out, pointing fingers our way, then loping toward us, teeth bared. One was Bradley, in his suit, distressingly persistent.

"Lil! Decide now, or forever hold your peace."

"But—"

"Tell me!"

"Oh—"

"Good grief. All right. Run!"

They flew up the narrow metal path into the yellow, mucoused sky, Jones faint with acrophobic visions through the grating.

"This would be a swell time to make up your mind, Lil."

"How can I? Why didn't you show up yesterday? Please stop. We've got to settle this."

"You mean discuss it?"

"Yes."

"But Lil. Oh, hell. Onto this scaffold. It may buy a moment or two."

It's a single seater sticky with red rustoleum, but it'll do for a cozy twosome. Careful, Lil, it's a mile down there and the water's hard. Try my lap and save the dress while I lower us among these rusty girders and small, spooky, whining winds. Lil, you're squeezing the brains out my ears. Down, girl.

"Fielding, I'm terrified."

"Let up a bit, Lil, I need to breathe. There's a catwalk below us. If we fall we may land on it."

"That's a comfort."

"You haven't sat on my lap for months, Lily. Remember the day we met?"

"This is hardly the time for nostalgia."

"You're right. It's strictly business. I love you, Lil."

"Jones!"

A voice of thunder from high above. I look, expecting clouds to crack, but discover it's only Bradley, tugging at the ropes.

"Arnold! Be careful or you'll kill us!"

"Lily. Dear, are you all right?"

"Arnold, I'm in love with Mr. Jones. What shall I do?"

Bradley's face turned florid as the sun beneath the bridge. "Lily! You don't know what you're saying. Come up here. Dammit, we're married."

"Lily."

"I love you, Fielding."

"Dammit, Lily! We've missed our plane to the Virgin

241

Islands! I won't let you do this!" Waving that same meaty fist. The cops are bewildered, staring down.

"Lil, may I ask you a very personal question?"

"I've gone and done it, Fielding."

"About last night . . ."

"Last night? I had a seizure."

"You mean he never . . ."

"No. Poor Arnold. All my life I'd feared it would happen just like that. It was horrible for both of us."

"Hahaha! A seizure! Beautiful! No entry, Bradley! Tough luck, old boy. Annulment in the morning!"

"Annulment like hell!" he shouted, wrenching up the rope. "Never, Jones!"

"Help, Fielding!"

"That man has a terrible temper, Lily. Good thing you found him out."

"Not 'til Doomsday, Jones!"

"Lil."

"Yes, Fielding."

"Do you lindy?"

"Do I what?"

"Oh, nothing."

There was a long, somber pause as down below the sinking sun licked the water into a genuine inferno. Lily held him tight about the neck.

"Do you think we'll be happy, Fielding?"

"Well, Lil, we'll try."

"Never!" roaring from above.

"Would you kiss me?"

"I will, Lily."

And hanging in the emptiness by a single line, spun by lonely winds like harmless spiders dangling in the tensile steel of their web, they touched uncertain lips, pressed them smiling, fearing, bosoms stuck tight and heaving like engines, as below them little flaming waves leapt up to see.

242

Walter Lockwood was born in St. Joseph, Michigan, on August 2, 1941, but has lived in Grand Rapids the greater part of his life. In 1963 he received a B.A. degree from Michigan State University Honors College, graduating with high honor. He attended Indiana University on a Woodrow Wilson fellowship and received his M.A. degree in English in 1964. At present he is working on a Ph.D. degree in American Studies at Michigan State University.

Mr. Lockwood has published stories in various little magazines, was a winner in the *Story* magazine national writing contest, and has had a story produced for television. He lives with his wife and three children in Grand Rapids, where he has taught English at Grand Rapids Junior College since 1965.